CAPPUCCINO MOMENTS

Pam Finch

Published by East Anglian Press
Copyright © Pam Finch 2015
ISBN: 978-0-9934934-1-6

British Library Cataloguing in Publication Data.
A CIP catalogue record for this book is available from the British Library.

Acknowledgements:

Many thanks to:

Suzan Collins of Get Writing who again has supported me to get my work written and published.

Richard and Gina of the Coconut Loft Art Gallery and Coffee Lounge for their continuing support.

Ellen of the Shed Café at the Henstead Arts & Crafts Centre for the photograph on the front cover.

The Waveney Author Group for their interest and encouragement.

CONTENTS

1st Story

I was balancing the spoon on the froth of my cappuccino waiting to see how long it took to sink.

'Do you mind if I sit here?'

I looked up. 'No. Please do.' I pulled my shopping off the chair onto the floor, 'It is busy in here today.'

He nodded an agreement, swung the chair out from the table, sat down and smiled. I liked his smile. He had obviously given his order at the counter as the waitress came across with a tray of tea.

'Don't need the milk, thank you,' he said. He smiled at the waitress. It really was a very nice smile. My spoon fell into the coffee; I took it out and licked it clean.

Making conversation he said, 'You look as though you've been busy shopping,'

'Yes. I have. Buying new bed linen for an aunt. Well, she's not really my aunt. Someone my mother knew when I was small and now she is just part of my life.'

'Oh dear.'

'No. She's lovely. Just a little too old to do some things for herself.'

He took the lid of the teapot and stirred his tea.

'You know, aunts can be strange creatures can't they?'

'Do you think so? 'I said.

'Most definitely. I remember a story my mother told me about an aunt.'

'Oh, yes?'

He poured out his tea. I looked at him, 'And …?'

He smiled and said:

"Aunt Dulcie …

Aunt Dulcie had a Sugar Daddy. It was Mr Bellamy who owned the Chemist shop. Aunt Dulcie was Mr Bellamy's shop assistant and from nine o'clock until six Aunt Dulcie's relationship with Mr Bellamy was strictly business. In her crisp white overall Aunt Dulcie would stand behind the glass cosmetic counter to administer to the town's crows' feet and lank hair. With her scarlet lips and glossy curls Mr Bellamy possessed a real life advertisement for his merchandise. Ladies craved to sample the latest shade of powder or try the newest face cream. While Aunt Dulcie was responsible to the customer's decorative wants, across the grey strip of rubberized matting, Mr Bellamy dealt with their prophylactic needs.

From her side of the shop Aunt Dulcie's bright brown eyes followed Mr Bellamy's dithering with the jars and phials of medication. They noticed how the pills fell haphazardly onto the brass tray scales; how with trembling hands Mr Bellamy rummaged through the row of oak drawers that stood behind his prescription counter.

Bottles of dreams and jars of desires were perhaps enough for most women, but Aunt Dulcie was ambitious, and was auditioning for a more demanding role than a shop assistant, and Mr Bellamy, as leading man would be expected to play his part and contribute to the success of her show.

Mr Bellamy was very generous to Aunt Dulcie: unbeknown to him, he was also very generous to Aunt Dulcie's family. Every Wednesday afternoon – early closing – she would visit her Mum, stay to tea, and catch the last bus back to her digs. Her two sisters, Ethel and Joan would also be there to squabble over tins of talcum powder, bottles of scent and extra fine hairnets that she had pinched from Mr Bellamy's shop.

Aunt Dulcie was always well dressed. Sitting at her mother's table surrounded by the purloined booty she stretched out an ample leg, hitch her skirt to show off 15 denier stockings. As she crossed her expensively sheened knee, attention would be drawn to the latest pair of suede sling backs; the peeped toes coyly exposing painted nails. She bought her costumes from "La Belle" in the High Street. Tight little jackets, nipped at the waist, with pencil slim skirts that hugged her backside. Some of the costumes had contrasting red or white lapels, or a flower arrangement attached to the shoulder, but always black.

'It shows taste,' said Aunt Dulcie.

Aunt Dulcie laughed a lot. The more tight-lipped her relatives, the more she opened her wide, naughty mouth. She would challenge their disapproval with puffs of *Craven A* that floated across the living room like Sioux messages. To the family it lingered as incomprehensible and alien as if it had been dispatched from the prairies.

So each Wednesday afternoon, there she would stand on the whitened step, provocatively rat-a-tatting the letter box, instead of going round to the kitchen door. She mischievously continued to clatter the knocker, aware of the fumbles on the other side. The front door would be opened at last by Ethel, who with a depressing smile, returned to the kitchen to light the gas under the kettle, leaving Aunt Dulcie to manage as best she could with her basket of contraband, a paper bag containing six Chelsea buns and an oversized crocodile-skin handbag – a grateful gift from Mr Bellamy. Once inside the hall, a deft kick from her platform sole and the front door slammed.

'It's only me,' she would sing out.

Aunt Dulcie's other sister, Joan, was married with two girls, and lived just a few streets from Mum. Every Wednesday afternoon she would wait impatiently at the school gate for her daughters to scurry them to Granny's. The sisters: ginger plaits and freckled stared mutely at Aunt Dulcie, who like a genie could conjure up the guilty gifts that were accepted with grudged willingness by their mother. A genie with a filter-tip drooping from shining lips and eye-lids that rhythmically closed as smoke curled from the lengthening ash. They marvelled at her hands – soft, smooth and white; plump little fingers tipped with nails like polished rubies. For the girls, the visits were exciting; after twitching their plaits Aunt Dulcie unscrewed a scent bottle, and dabbed the smell behind their ears. In reply to their mother's outraged sniff, Aunt Dulcie would shrug a shoulder and give a long, slow wink to the sisters.

To Aunt Dulcie, this mid-week escapade was by way of a dress rehearsal to a star performance. Lipsticks and the occasional Home Perm were trifles, for not only did Mr Bellamy own the Chemist Shop, he also owned a luxury service flat overlooking the park; some run-down properties near the railway station; a large bank balance and a dicky heart.

To her relatives, the fearful implications of this pilfering hung over them from one week to the next like a doomed cloud ready to burst a deluge of disgrace and retribution on their heads, but regularly each Wednesday, Aunt Dulcie and the swag came to tempt and regularly each Wednesday she succeeded. Aunt Dulcie brought a whiff of decadence to the tea-party and to the other women it was both fascinating and frightening; their proximity to wickedness on Wednesdays excited their dull routine, though Thursdays brought trepidation.

It was the Wednesday following Easter that Aunt Dulcie never arrived. By the time Ethel's after-dinner chores were over, she knew it must be nearly half past two. When she finally went into the living room and looked at the mantelpiece, the clock showed a quarter to three, and the nervous, hollow pains in her ribs and upper arms were getting worse. She returned to the kitchen, jerked Vim into the sink and scoured at imaginary stains. The cold water bounced angrily out of the sink as Mum came into the kitchen, lifted the empty kettle from the stove, held it mid-air for a moment, returned it to the unlit gas ring and said:

'It's ten past.'

Ethel wrenched the water off, twisted the dish cloth dry, uncoiled it with a vicious whip and flung it over the tap. As Mum left the kitchen, Ethel threw more Vim onto the draining board, and gripping the scrubbing brush with both hands, started to savage the wood.

When Joan and the girls clattered through the back door at five past four, the cold kitchen gave them the first indication that this was not going to be a typical Wednesday visit. The kettle was not boiling, nor was the tea tray ready. Joan's first thought was Mum, but in the living room Mum was sitting, as usual, by the fire. The unusual was Ethel perched on the arm of the other easy chair: feet, knees, hands and lips clamped together. Both women were staring at the little pile of smouldering coals. Joan looked at the dining table; the embroidered runner, with its ironed creases, stretched diagonally across the polished surface emphasised the empty afternoon.

'Not here then?'

The question, neither wanted, nor needed brought the women's thoughts together and set them like a plate of unappetising food on the table. The young sisters, blocked out of the room by their mother's hips, tried to squeeze into the drama. Their mother turned, bundled them through the kitchen and into the back yard.

Had she an accident? Been knocked down?

Each woman visualised the scene the basket. The victim a blurred, black huddle. In their mind's eye each could see, with horrid clarity the strewn contents of the basket. Irrefutable evidence that would ultimately find its way to Number 36 Darby Street. Ethel silently totted up the tins of *"Lily of the Valley"* talc packed under her knickers in the chest of drawers and prayed. Joan thought about the girls and felt hot tingles round her midriff as she recalled the strong smell of *"Midnight in Paris"*. Mum was not perturbed; she was old; she would deny everything.

Cups of tea were eventually drunk, and a plate of Marie biscuits passed desultorily round the room. The girls were allowed in and lolled against their mother's lap; their unsoiled ears, cold, pink and cocked.

The accident theory was replaced by conjecture over a cold? Sore throat? That in turn was dismissed for Ethel's contribution of a bus strike, but the combined glare from Joan and Mum had it immediately crossed from the agenda. Joan eventually demanded twenty minutes suspension in order to return her daughters to their own chaste home, placate Bert and light the gas under his stew.

'Don't do anything until I get back,' she warned.

By a quarter past seven the word couldn't be ignored any longer. They had skirted round it; ducked under it; leapt over it. Now as they sat round the dining table, it hovered over them like a taunting, uninvited spirit at a séance.

'Arrested.' It was Joan who said it, 'That's what's happened. She been and got herself arrested.'

The finality of the statement brought relief and each of the women began to make her own private plans to prove her neutrality in the imminent scandal that was about to encircle Aunt Dulcie.

***

Aunt Dulcie hasn't got a Sugar Daddy any more. Aunt Dulcie has got a husband. That Wednesday as Ethel was assaulting the draining board, Aunt Dulcie, resplendent in a new costume, new high heels, new gloves and wearing the latest pill-box complete with spotted veil, was clinging to the arm of Mr Bellamy. There they stood, the happy couple on the steps of the Registry Office, opposite the undertakers. Aunt Dulcie carried her bouquet – a sheaf of orange tea roses – with the aplomb of a prima donna acknowledging a standing ovation. At home as the women had waited, watching the slow tormenting hands of the clock, on the pavement the photographer waited patiently as Aunt Dulcie searched her new pig skin handbag for her new compact – both grateful gifts from Mr Bellamy. While the family sat in tense conference in the living room, Aunt Dulcie snuggled up to Mr Bellamy as their car whisked them on honeymoon. She pressed a powdered cheek against Mr Bellamy's lapel and crushed his red carnation.

At a quarter past seven the Residents' Bar of the Drayton Hotel was warm, smokey and ready for a long evening of indulgence. As that awful word was being uttered at Number 36 Darby Street, Mr and Mrs Bellamy walked into the bar, sat themselves comfortably on the high stools and ordered. Mrs Bellamy was in sequins. Mr Bellamy lifted his whiskey.

'Here's to us, dearie.'

His wife picked up her gin and orange, held it level to her eye and winked through the glass.

'Bottoms Up,' said Aunt Dulcie."

I shook my head, 'Haven't got any aunts like that in my family.'

He smiled and poured himself a second cup of tea.

*

2nd Story

I dunked only a third of my biscuit into the coffee, took it out and ate it. Success. As I was carefully dipping the biscuit again, a stack of books fell first on the table and then to the floor.

'Sorry. I'm so sorry.'

I looked up at him: 'No worries, but you are rather laden.'

He untucked two more books from under his arm, put them on the chair and gathered up those that had fallen.

He said, 'I do apologise. Should have got myself a bag.'

'Men don't like to carry bags.'

He smiled. 'I know. Vain, aren't we?'

The waitress stood by the table. I looked down at the tiny corner of the biscuit I was holding; the rest had disappeared through the froth of my cappuccino.

He ordered his tea and said, 'May I?'

'Of course.'

He sat down and I glanced at the titles of his books. They were all about sailing ships.'

'Do you sail?' I asked.

'Not anymore, but I'm researching the history of wherries.'

'Wherries? I've heard about them.'

'Yes wonderful crafts'.

The waitress came with his tea.

'Tell me about them.'

He took the lid off the pot and stirred the tea.

'Please,' I said.

He smiled and said:

"The River …

This is about a wherry, but more importantly it is a story about a river. A river that caused rivalry as it was the boundary that separated two counties.

***

'Ellen?'

'Yes Mother?'

'Remember what to tell Cousin Sarah?'

'Yes Mother.'

Ellen swung the basket as she walked between the lavender bushes to the gate.

'Mind the eggs.'

'Yes Mother.'

Once out of sight of the cottage, Ellen continued to swing the basket; each time a little higher – she' never yet broken an egg.

She hummed to herself as she walked along the lane out of the village. Days like this were wonderful. A bright sky, tiny clouds, just a breeze. She kicked up little puffs of dust, then remembering Cousin Sarah, stopped when she reached the bridge and rubbed the toe of each boot with the hem of her skirt. When Ellen was halfway across the bridge, she shaded her eyes and peered upstream. The river shone in the morning light. Wherries were being unloaded next to the maltings, but she couldn't see Tom. She crossed to the other side of the bridge and looked down river for a black sail. No. Nothing. She continued over the bridge, still swinging the basket. Cousin Sarah lived in one of the first cottages past the bridge; in the other county. As she pushed open the yard gate, Ellen heard voices. One was Cousin Sarah's and the other was … Ellen groaned … Willy, or William as Cousin Sarah insisted on him being called. Ellen stepped into the kitchen.

'Hello Willy. Not at work?'

Ellen watched the exchanged glance between Cousin Sarah and her son.

'Now Ellen, you know William has a weak chest. That stuffy office does not do it any good at all. His father keeps having words with the owner, but the hours that man expects William to be at his desk is ridiculous.'

Cousin Sarah fetched a large basin from the dresser for the eggs and from the mantelpiece an old biscuit tin; she shook some coppers onto the table. Ellen scooped up the money.

'Mother said to tell you she will bring the eggs next week.'

Cousin Sarah sniffed; shrugged her shoulders. 'Is she indeed? Crossing the bridge? Coming into our county? Well. Well.'

Willy let out a high pitched laugh. Ellen glared at him and the young man pulled at his stiff collar.

'Are you staying and having a piece of my seed cake?'

'Sorry Cousin Sarah, but I have to get home.' Ellen stepped out into the yard.

'Wait, William can manage to walk a little way with you. You two must get to know each other a little better.' Cousin Sarah beamed and Ellen frowned.

'Why are you walking so fast?' William's voice had a whine to it that Ellen found particularly annoying. She ignored the question and quickened her step. William said:

'Mother is right, you know?'

'Right about what?'

'Well, you are quite a nice little thing – though you ... '

Ellen spun round and faced the young man.

'Though I what?'

'Errh,' William took off his bowler hat and rubbed his hand across his forehead, 'You've got a lot to learn.'

His pompous tone encouraged Ellen.

'And you Willy, sorry William, are the person to teach me?'

'Yes, I believe I could. But to begin with, you would have to give up all this nonsense I hear about you spending so much time by the river.'

'I love the river.'

'Love the river? That's rather an absurd statement.'

'But I do – 1 love it – I love how it moves. How sometimes it dashes along so fast it makes foamy waves and then another time the surface just wriggles and ripples like ... like silk. I love where it's wide and grand, and then it bends and curves. I love its colours; sometimes so deep and dark, it's black and then this morning, it was sparkling.'

'Sparkling! What sort of a word is that for a river?'

They had reached the bridge and Ellen ran ahead leaned against the iron parapet.

'Hurry up,' she called.

'I don't think I wish to come any further.'

'What's the matter? Are you scared?' She dropped her voice and croaked, 'Are you scared of the river, Willy?'

'That's another of your absurd statements.'

'Or are you too frightened to step into my county. Oooooooo.'

William said, 'You really are a silly person.'

Ellen ignored the remark and said: 'Come here and look. Oh, please look.'
William walked slowly and stood by her side. She pointed to a wherry that had just appeared from the bend, down river.

'It's the *Kingfisher* and Tom.'

'The what?'

'*The Kingfisher*. Tom and his father work the *Kingfisher*. Oh, I so hoped they would be here today.'

Ellen watched William nervously edge a little closer to the parapet.

'How do you know it's the *Kingfisher*? All wherries look the same.'

'They don't. They don't. Look it's got a white masthead.'

'So?'

'So,' Ellen blew out a sigh, 'A white masthead with blue and green bands means ... it's the *Kingfisher*.

Ellen put her boot into one of the lattice holes of the parapet and hoisted herself up.

'Tom. Tom-e-e-e-e.' she shouted.

'I think I had better return home,' said William hugging the bowler hat to his chest.

'Just watch,' said Ellen, 'Just watch the *Kingfisher* shoot through the bridge.'

The wherry was now about a hundred yards from the bridge. Ellen could see Tom laying aside the quant; the tide was pushing them upstream. The mainsheet was being gathered in for lowering, then sail and gaff came down at a run. Ellen watched Tom jump onto the hatch. She heard him call:

'Pin out. Heave away.'

The wherry came closer.

Ellen climbed another rung of the parapet and balancing forward waved her basket with one hand and her straw hat with the other.

'Tom-e-e-e-e. It's m-e-e-e-e.'

A voice was heard: 'Lower your mast.'

Ellen watched the mast slightly sway then swing down into a graceful arc and rest over the hatch.

'Do we have an understanding then? Mother thinks we should.'

Ellen turned. 'Willy. This is important.'

'My sentiments exactly,' he replied putting on his bowler.

At that moment the *Kingfisher* slid under the bridge. Tom's tanned face looked up at Ellen and he grinned, 'See you up at the quay.'

Ellen jumped down and ran across the road to the other parapet. William stood in the middle of the road. The wherry was now clear of the bridge and the mast swung upright. The mid-morning breeze had got a little stronger and as the sail was hoisted the *Kingfisher* smoothly glided upstream. Ellen climbed again the lattice rungs – one, two, three … at that moment there was a shout from William, and Ellen saw the bowler hat being tossed by the wind over the parapet. William ran and climbed up beside Ellen. They both watched the bowler drop into the river and bob along in the wake of the wherry. William turned to Ellen.

'Stop laughing you foolish young woman. It's all your fault.'

As he spoke, he shot his arm in the direction of the *Kingfisher*; he wanted to attract the attention of Tom; but with the abrupt movement he lost his balance and Ellen watched as he tumbled into the river. The splash and Ellen's scream brought Tom to the stern of the wherry. Ellen ran over the bridge and along the towpath. William had surfaced; he was waving and gurgling. Ellen heard another splash and saw Tom swimming towards him. Men at work on the tannery jetty shouted advice. Ellen knelt down close to the reeds at the water's edge. She heard Tom telling William not to struggle. Once Tom had William near the bank, Ellen grabbed his coat and with Tom pushing and Ellen pulling they got him out of the river. Tom slapped William a couple of times between the shoulder blades. When William had finished coughing he said:

'My bowler hat. My new bowler hat. Did you get it?'

Tom was wringing water from his shirt. 'No, bor. That I didn't.'

'Really; it's all too bad.' He turned to Ellen. 'You are to blame you know.'

Ellen ignored the remark and dried her hands on the grass. William stood up; pulled at his heavy wet jacket; his boots made a sucking noise as stepped around the bank.

'Oh, Willy, do you know what has happened?'

'No I don't. And it's William.'

'Well, William. You've come over the border. You're in my county now.'

Ellen sat back on her heels, glanced at Tom and started to laugh."

He poured out his tea and smiled, and I smiled back.

*

3rd Story

I looked at my cappuccino. No sprinkles. I glanced across the coffee shop and tried to catch the waitress's eye, but she was busy wedging the door shut. Just as she managed to get it closed it crashed open again and he rushed in. He helped the waitress close the door, came over to my table and sat down.

'Gosh, what a day, he said.

'I know and rain is forecast for later.'

His tea was brought over.

'Yes,' he smiled, 'I heard we are due for a severe storm.'

I said, 'I hope not like the one in – now what year was it? Caused all that damage.'

'Mmm,' he poured out his tea. 'Mmm.'

'What are you thinking about?' I asked.

He picked up his cup.

'You've got a story for me, haven't you?'

He smiled and said:

"From Little Acorns …

He thought: Thank God the day was nearly over. Been nothing but arguments; problems; incompetence and now rain. Paul Turner, age thirty-seven, waist forty-three, increased the rhythm of the wipers and unconsciously increased his speed. The arcs dried for a moment before the windscreen speckled again with rain. Ahead, the juggernaut appeared distorted, its rear lights blurred as the wheels threw spray from the road. Paul Turner, married with a spreading bald patch, glanced in the mirror – headlights seemed comfortably distant - flicked the indicator, accelerated and overtook. The outraged blast, either from the juggernaut or the following car screamed above the slushing wheels. Paul Turner, father of three boys whose birthdays he could not remember, acknowledged the sound with two indicator flashes.

Immediately, standing out of the grey evening was the square green sign, and the irritable driving subsided, the car slowed and took the exit for Bournemouth. During the next few miles the rain eased. Paul Turner, the Senior Sales Representative (London & South Coast), promotion to Marketing Director imminent, relaxed and watched for the lay-by. As he pulled in, the rain suddenly increased and drummed on the car roof; impatient he tattooed his fingers on the steering wheel waiting. Then the sky brightened; with the back of his hand he cleaned a dry circle on the screen. He waited a moment more then took out his mobile.

'Hello.'

'Ben? It's Dad. Mummy there?'

He pulled the phone away from his ear as the receiver was dropped onto a table. The faint "Mummy" could be heard calling over the mumbling of the television's early evening news.

'Paul?'

'Look Jemma, 'fraid I won't get back tonight.'

'Oh.'

'Sorry.'

'Where are you?'

'London.'

'Oh.'

'Sorry.'

'Whereabouts?'

'Off the North Circular. B&B. Grotty little place.'

'Oh, Paul. Well, never mind. What time will you be home tomorrow?'

'Hard to say. 'Bout this time I should think.'

'Right.'

'Better go. Lots to do. Say "Night-night" to the boys.'

'Yes. Right. Bye love.'

***

Paul Turner blinked awake and listened. Nothing. He put his chin over the duvet and glanced round the charcoal dark room. He looked over to the dressing table; the triple mirror multiplied the familiar shadowy reflections. He dropped his head into the pillow's warm dip and turned over. He stretched his legs down the cool sheets, then pulled his knees up and formed an identical body curve round his sleeping mistress. He savoured the duvet cosy about his ears as his mind performed the tricky combination of simultaneously floating and sinking ...

The roar smashed into the double glazing. The cocooned couple turned as one. Flat on their backs they waited.

'What's that?'

'Dunno.'

The next roar filled the bedroom.

'Paul!'

Rachel's hand reached under the covers.

'God's sake, Rach.'

'What is it?'

'Your damn nails.'

'No. The noise. What is it?'

The roaring continued. It thudded and vibrated from the walls; then dropped into a heavy silence; the stillness more ominous in the leaden room. The pair waited.

'Paul. Paul.'

'Wh-a-a.'

'What was it? Put the light on, do.'

He sat up slowly, the duvet slid away from Rachel's shoulders. She snatched at it – too quickly and he lost his balance and flopped back onto the pillow.

'Hurry up. Put the light on.'

Then again another roar, a solid, dense noise.

'Okay. Shuup.'

The bad-tempered whisper was pitched above the noise, so that when it again suddenly ceased, his voice came barking at her from the edge of the bed. He said:

'It's the wind.'

'Can't be.'

'It is. Listen.'

Rachel rested up on her elbow. 'Put the light on.'

'Can't find the switch.'

'It's there.'

'Not working.'

'Try the main light.'

He fumbled across the room to the door. The wallpaper felt cold as he ran his hand looking for the switch. The roaring increased again; its volume seemed capable of injury.

'No,'

'What do you mean?'

'What I say. No electricity.'

'Can't be.'

Rachel hated not knowing what was happening. Draping the duvet over her shoulders she went and stood by the window.

There was no moon. No street lights. She stared into the night and waited until her eyes gradually could see the outline of the houses on the other side of the road. She was aware that away from the nullifying effect of the double bed, extra sounds penetrated the roaring wind. The pavement trees creaked as the trunks fought against the abnormal buffeting; garden fences scraped from broken posts and the neighbour's metal gate grated and clanked as it first violently swung open and shut, over and over again. Roof slates clattered onto the road; the sound echoing sharply when they hit the parked cars. Screaming along the road were torn branches and battered garden shrubs. An assortment of debris hurled past Rachel's house. In one of the frightening lulls she became aware of a more familiar sound. She pushed the curtains away from her face.

'What are you grumbling about?'

'Where's the blasted duvet?'

'Here. I've got it.'

Rachel left the window as an intermittent hollow cracking sound pushed through the roaring. Rachel moved towards the bed dragging the duvet from her shoulders. As she lifted her knee onto the mattress, the cracking became a continuous rent – with it a rumbling. The noise seemed directly above the bed. The rumbling intensified, shoving the roaring into the corners of the room.

Rachel screamed, 'Paul.'

He pulled her into the centre of the bed.

'Quick. Come here.'

His instinct was sharpened by the inability to see. A lump of plaster landed on his bare buttocks. He crammed her into a huddle under him and was trying to fling the duvet over their bodies when the ceiling cracked and split into dozens of pieces. Leaves appeared first through the crumbling plaster; their topaz, copper and gold autumn colours clogged with powdered cement and brick dust. Branches fell into the room together with the rubble from smashed tiles, broken joists and fragments of stone and brick.

For a brief moment, that afterwards seemed like their entire past life, the couple were then aware of a coolness; a feeling of fresh air blowing in the room. The unexpectedness of the cold made them fearful because it was so natural, and they realized what had happened, and what was to follow, and they could only crouch together on the mattress as it took place. As the cold surrounded their bodies, they felt their mouths go dry; they couldn't breathe. The bedroom began to fill with dust and grit. They were being stifled. They both felt pains in their ribs as though a vice was squeezing air out of their lungs. They gripped their arms around each other for protection.

The oak tree crashed first onto the wardrobe. As the pinewood doors buckled and splintered, the tree lurched towards the dressing table, hitting the corner. It rocked there for a moment, then slowly and elegantly, it toppled and fell onto the double bed.

***

Paul Turner's sons had finished their tea. The youngest boy, excluded from a particularly rough bout of wrestling in progress behind the sofa, scrawled over the carpet hunting for lost building bricks. Having found a few pieces, he knelt back on his feet and concentrated on fixing them together. In the corner, the television reported the early evening news. The boy studied his plastic construction and called to the kitchen for praise. Jemma Turner left the washing up, came into the living room, stood still and stared. The boy looked at his mother and realized she was ignoring his handiwork. He followed her gaze to the television screen. The newscaster was reporting the freak storm that had hit the south coast the night before.

All during the day there had been reports of the devastation – numbers dead and injured; flattened buildings; disruptive services. Now, as in all disasters, stories of heroism, fortitude and inspiration were trickling through the overall misery...

Jemma Turner screamed, and there, in a flicker of a moment, she watched her husband being carried bloodied, broken, but alive from the ruins of a Bournemouth house. As Jemma followed the dramatic coloured pictures, she saw instead her own grey desolate future. The storm had not reached out to harm them. Their house was unscathed, but the pleasure of their home was demolished. Trees were still growing in her Lancashire garden, but her love had been uprooted and tossed aside. Around her, Jemma's possessions were unspoiled, but none of them could shield her from an indifference that would destroy her life. Jemma's mouth was dry and she could not breathe. She was being stifled. The pain in her ribs felt as though a vice was squeezing the air out of her lungs. She gripped her arms together for protection and stumbled into a chair. The wrestlers peered out from behind the sofa.

Clinging to the stretcher, a blanket covering her nakedness was Paul Turner's tearful and grimed stained mistress. Rachel noticed the reporter, then the camera: wide eyed she looked into the lens and straight at Jemma Turner and said: 'His love saved my life.' "

'Oh.' I sighed, 'A sad story for miserable day.'
'Sorry.'

*

4th Story

The tiny sachet was sitting in my saucer. I picked it up, shook it and naturally had trouble tearing it open.

'Hi. Problems?'

What's this?' I asked him

He sat down. 'A chocolate coffee bean.'

'Oh,' I said.

The sachet split and the tiny brown bean fell, rolled across the floor and stopped by the counter.

As the waitress put down his tea he asked ,'Do you work?'

'Part-time.'

'Sorry. Shouldn't be inquisitive.'

'No. It's fine. I help out for a few hours a week at the college library.'

'Coincidence,' he smiled.

'You're not there are you? I haven't seen you.'

'No. No. Another town; another college; another library.'

'Oh.'

He looked at me.

I drank a little of my cappuccino and said, 'I'm waiting,'

'For what?'

'Don't tease. Work with books and you haven't got a story.'

He smiled and said:

"Such Special Words …

Abbie felt pleased with herself. She had wanted to drive the rural library van ever since she started her job as an assistant librarian and now, thanks to Steve's cold, she had finally got the chance.

Abbie checked the rear-view mirror, decided she had parked in the correct place by the Green, and pulled up the handbrake. She clambered out of the seat and swung open the double doors. She then re-stacked the books that had fallen from the shelves on the last bumpy stretch of road into the village. After that she checked the date stamp, tried it out on the ink-pad and sharpened some pencils. Abbie sighed contentedly; no sitting in front of a computer screen today – hurrah! She peeped out of the doors, looking first up past the church, then back towards the cross-roads. No one. Well, it was early and spitting with rain. Abbie busied herself changing the Romantic Fiction shelf with the Crime and Adventure, then the Supernatural with Hobbies. She then thought Steve would not be pleased and changed them all back again. She looked at her watch. Five more minutes then she must leave. She was closing the doors when she saw him running towards the van. He was carrying a purple and orange striped umbrella and waving a book.

'Thanks. Thought I'd missed you.'

He closed the umbrella and propped it by the door. He saw Abbie looking at it. 'It's Grandma's.'

Abbie took the book and checked the return date.

'Do you want to choose another book?' she asked

'Grandma said you always choose for her.'

'Me?'

'Yes. She said you always pick the books she likes.'

'No. Not me. Must be Steve. I'm the relief, but let me see what you have returned.'
Abbie picked up the book again.

'Mmm. "*A Kung Fu Killing*". I'll have a look.'

As she placed the book on the shelf a book-mark fell on the floor.

'Here. This must be your Grandma's'

He took it and said: '*You Are Beautiful*'.

'Pardon?' said Abbie.

'The book-mark. Grandma makes them when she is not reading murder mysteries.'

Abbie looked at the stitched words surrounded by embroidered daisies.

'Very pretty. How about "*A Messy Massacre*"?

He grinned. 'Sounds right to me.'

Abbie scanned the library card, opened the book and stamped the date. As she handed him the book she studied the sun-burnt face and fair hair.

'Everything okay?' he asked.

'Oh, yes, yes,' replied Abbie shuffling together pieces of scrap paper for something to do.

He tucked the book under his arm, picked up the umbrella and jumped from the van.

'Thanks for your help.'

'You're welcome,' said Abbie and closed the doors.

As Steve's cold turned into a sore throat, two weeks later Abbie on a cool, windy day was again parked by the Green. Again she waited patiently and was about to close the van doors when she saw him hurrying along the road.

'Nearly didn't make it,' he laughed, 'Only arrived at Grandma's few minutes ago. "Be quick," she said, "you must change my library book".'

As he handed Abbie the book, a book-mark dropped to the floor; he picked it up, glanced at the embroidered words and said: '*I Love You*'.

Abbie turned away and looked along the shelves.

'There's "*An Awful Assassination*" or "*A Shocking Slaughter*"?'

He smiled. 'Better make it the "*Assassination*".'

Abbie scanned the library card, stamped the book and handed it to him. Never, thought Abbie, had she seen such blue eyes.

*****

Abbie watched the lightly falling snow through the windscreen. She was worried about Steve, now on extended sick leave. She had been parked for about ten minutes when there was a knock on the van doors. When Abbie opened them a middle-aged woman stepped in.

'Good morning,' she said and handed Abbie a book. Abbie glanced at the title: "*An Awful Assassination*".

'My neighbour's,' explained the woman, 'Housebound – and that grandson of hers has gone back to Australia.'

Abbie put the book on the shelf.

'I said: "Don't worry dear. Leave it to me. I know what sort of book you would like".'

The woman spent some time browsing.

'Here we are,' she said at last.

She handed Abbie the book. The title was "*Dreams of Romance.*"

'I think that will be suitable,' she continued.

Abbie stamped the book.

After she had gone, Abbie, putting the returned book on the shelf noticed a book-mark wedged between the covers. It was embroidered with buttercups and Abbie smiled as she read the yellow silk words, before she put it away in the pencil drawer.

***

Steve got better and Abbie went back to work at her computer in the town library.

It was the following April; Steve decided on a spring holiday so Abbie took the rural library van back to the village. She parked by the Green, opened the doors, sat on the steps in the sunshine and waited. She watched him come along past the church, pause for a moment, then start to run towards the van, waving a book. He's back, thought Abbie.

'You're back,' he said, 'Great.'

Abbie took the book and put it on the counter.' What shall it be? Another murder?'

'No hurry,' he said, 'Is there?'

Abbie shook head. He sat down on the van steps and Abbie sat beside him. She listened while he told her about the dusty town in Queensland where he worked, and about the beach holidays in Sydney. He told her about his Grandma who wanted him to come and live near her.

'I think I will,' he said, 'My work with computers allows me to work where I want.'

'Ugh! Computers!' said Abbie and told him of her days at the library watching a screen, instead of handling the old beautiful books that she loved. She told him her name was Abbie, short of Abigail; that she loved strawberry ice-cream and had a black cat called Twitch.

He told her that his name was Joe – not short for anything; that he had a married sister in Edinburgh and hated Peppermint Creams.

Abbie looked at her watch and jumped up. She went to the shelves and ran her fingers along the spines trying to decide on a book for Grandma. She chose one and turned. Joe was standing by her side.

'What about "*A Dreadful Death*"?' she asked.

He went to take the book and his hands covered hers.

'It will do fine. By the way Grandma seems to think she left a book-mark in one of the books ages ago.'

Abbie pulled her hands away and opened the pencil drawer. She pushed aside rubber bands, paper clips and a broken date stamp until she found the book-mark. She blew dust from it and handed it to him.

'Thanks.'

Abbie opened the ink-pad.

'Have you read it?' asked Joe.

'What … this book?'

'No. The book-mark.'

'Er … no,' Abbie tried to shrug.

'Shall I read it to you?'

Abbie looked up into the blue eyes.

'Do you want to?'

'I most certainly do.'

He took Abbie's hand, then picking up the book-mark read *'Please Be My Sweetheart'*.

Abbie looked at Joe and said:

'Yes Joe I will. After I've stamped Grandma's book.' "

'Ah, young love,' I said.

He smiled, and I heard the crunch as the waitress stood on the bean.

*

5th Story

I was having trouble getting the little biscuit out of its wrapping. Then the cellophane suddenly split and the biscuit fell into my cappuccino.

'You're having problems,' he said.

By the time he had pulled off his gloves and unwound his scarf, his tea had arrived. He sat down and poured it out immediately.

'Surely you like it stronger,' I said.

He leaned back in the chair and sighed: 'Yes I know, but I'm desperate.'

'Why? What have you been doing? Sorry I shouldn't pry.'

'Please do. I've been visiting my mother – she's in Larkspur Lodge. I've just sat there for an hour and a half holding her skeins of wool, but I feel exhausted.'

To hide my smile, I busied myself again with the now floating biscuit crumbs.

'She just doesn't stop talking ...'

'Well,' I interrupted, 'She must look forward to your visits. I always think it must be a bit boring in those Residential Homes.'

I chased the soggy biscuit round the cup, then gave up.

'Huh – Boring? he said, 'You'd never believe it. Do you know what she told me today?'

'No. What?'

He drained his cup and poured out another, smiled and said:

"Pecking Order ...

From the table in the centre of the dining room someone was missing. An empty chair: evidence of either incompetence, mis-management or both. The three people seated at the table looked towards the swing doors – they remained closed. Of the three, only Miss Hall felt guilty. Guilty of contributing to a breakdown of house rules. She should have waited, but hunger had beaten hospitality. She looked at her two companions; they concentrated on munching. All around them inquisitive conversations first began to simmer, then bubble. Staff weaved between tables with trays of crockery and plates of food. The meal continued; laps filled with crumbs; tea slopped onto the table clothes and the speculative chattering returned to slow simmering.

On her right, Elsie was fumbling. Miss Hall flicked her a glance and the fumbling became more agitated as Elsie tried to open her dusty handbag. The clasp was stiff for her arthritic fingers. Just as she was about to abandon the activity, and resume it at bedtime, the clasp wilfully gave way and the bag opened. In her surprise Elsie relinquished the strap and three safety pins, an empty crochet purse and a string of plastic beads first tumbled amongst the folds of her skirt, then slowly skittered onto the floor. Elsie flung out her left arm for balance as she listed starboard from her chair in an endeavour to trawl in some of her treasures. Surfacing due to dizziness, her flaying arm caught the back of Miss Hall's chair and knocked the lady's two ebony walking sticks to the ground. The sticks took their time to fall. The noise before they finally hit the polished parquet was reminiscent of an under rehearsed Morris dance.

The third occupant of this undisciplined table was a gentleman. Harry looked down at the walking sticks behind Miss Hall's chair and sighed. He searched for an authoritative overall, but those on duty were huddled over an argument near the window He sighed again as he resentfully became aware of the first shaft of dyspepsia. Checking the floor's surface, he pushed down his slippered feet as he raised his backside; at the same time ambitiously attempting to slide his chair away with the backs of his legs. He knew it was not going to be a success the moment he placed his hands on the corners of the table for extra leverage.

Miss Hall kept her deceptively faded blue eyes closed as she waited for the crash. It was the sound of breaking crockery that enabled the missing occupant of the now defunct table to locate the dining room. Mrs Betty Anderson, newly arrived resident of the Larkspur Lodge for the Elderly had felt confident, when half an hour earlier she had been shown a chair in the communal lounge; also relieved to see it was devoid of the obligatory rainbow-knitted blanket. She had been introduced to her comatose neighbour whose chair effectively blocked the television screen and the pale heat from the imitation coal fire. Flanking the other side, and obstructing a safe passage to the magazine trolley by extending two walking sticks well beyond the chair's allocated perimeter, sat another resident. Mrs Anderson thought they were about to be introduced when another member of staff began to herd everyone along a corridor to the dining room for tea. Mrs Anderson went, as was natural to wash her hands. When she returned to the lounge it was deserted and she had lost all sense of direction.

Concerned and hurrying as quickly as her walking frame would allow Mrs Anderson eventually found the dining room. Once through the swing doors the staff's amnesia as to her existence was immediately overcome when they saw her patiently waiting by an alcove and she was escorted to the hub of the dwindling drama. The collapsed table, now upright had been covered with another paper cloth. Broken china and crusts had been carted away and Harry's trousers sponged. Miss Hall's walking sticks were hanging sulkily from the back of her chair again. The other residents who had finished eating were reluctantly being led away to watch a games show on television.

The initiative of the kitchen staff produced a plate of quartered sandwiches for Mrs Anderson, and as a palliative to the trauma, a carnival of iced buns; besides the unprecedented decision of allowing the table its own brown china teapot. A diminutive member of staff with earrings the size of saucepan lids rested on the walking frame whilst Mrs Anderson slowly negotiated her chair. Once seated, Mrs Anderson looked around at her teatime companions.

Elsie was staring at the iced buns, hoping she would be quick enough for the yellow one – she was sure it was lemon flavoured. Miss Hall graciously nodded her head; then graciously smiled as she edged the plate of buns a fraction towards the newcomer. The gesture indicating despite the arrival of a well-cut skirt and jacket, to say nothing of the expensive coiffure, her role as head of the table, was to remain unchallenged. Harry gloomily eyes the iced buns – although he could anticipate a night of acidity, he felt he had more than earned himself a treat. The lemon flavoured one was his fancy.

'Good afternoon,' said Mrs Anderson. She studied the plate of iced buns and thought: What a garish selection; it will have to be the lemon one or nothing. Harry feebly punched his weekday tie a few inches below the loose knot and the burning penetrated through to his shoulder blades. Mrs Anderson lightly touched his arm.

'Indigestion?' she murmured.

Harry turned and his look of annoyance disappeared and fellow suffers exchanged conspiratorial sympathy.

Miss Hall was re-arranging the crockery prior to pouring. She had overseen Elsie, Harry and the recently departed Mrs Watson ever since arriving at "Larkspur" two years ago, but never had she been custodian of a tea-pot. Today's humiliating fiasco had been the latest in a trail of mishaps over which she had unfortunately presided, but with the prestige of a tailor costume, complete with gold and pearl lapel brooch, a more civilised attitude at meal times might well be achieved. The tea-pot was the first step in the right direction. Also to consolidate her position she would make in known, when she had finished pouring, that her choice of cake was the lemon-flavoured one.

It was as Miss Hall lifted the tea-pot, full and ready to overflow into the first cup that her concentration failed due to etiquette. Here at last was the opportunity, as hostess, for which she had been patiently waiting. This latest resident's social standing would understand and appreciate Miss Hall's polite enquiry. The words: 'I know you would prefer to add your own milk' were being elegantly formed in her mind, practised for the correct intonation in order to suggest like minded manners. Such a query would only have encouraged an uncouth grunt from Harry; bewildered splashing by Elsie; and to have made old Mrs Watson understand, the necessary shouting would have vibrated around the room, bounced off the walls before being lost with 'Pardon, dear?'

Miss Hall was ready to enunciate the phrase. If Miss Hall had not been watching the slanting spout she would, no doubt, have looked at the plate of iced buns, and could possibly have taken evasive action.

Elsie's hand fluttered over the table like a nervous sparrow trying to land in Trafalgar Square, as Harry's paw lunged from the opposite direction. But neither was as quick as Mrs Anderson's small manicured fingers. The coveted yellow bun has been plucked from the table centre and placed on her own plate, minus a half-moon bite, while the established tea-timers were still jostling for position. The imminent tea sloshed back down the spout as Miss Hall crashed the tea-pot onto the table. Mrs Anderson smiled again.

'Rheumatism love? Let me.' Her arm shot across the table and gripping the tea-pot handle she filled the four cups; placing the empty pot next to her elbow.

'I'll put in our milk, shall I?'

Harry grunted; Elsie giggled and Miss Hall sank.

'There,' continued Mrs Anderson. She lifted the sugar bowl with one hand, the tongs with the other.

'Now. Who's for a sugar lump?' "

I looked at him; he smiled and said, 'I'm going to have to order another pot of tea.'

*

6th Story

I was poking around in the sugar bowl looking for a brown lump amongst all the white ones; I found one and dropped it onto froth and waited for it to sink.

'Hello,' he said.

I looked at him, 'My, you have been shopping.'

He put the bags down on the empty chair. I read the gold lettering of the name of the High Street tailors.

'Bought a new suit?'

'Yes, and shirt and waistcoat and tie. For a wedding.'

'Yours?'

He smiled and sat down opposite me. 'Ooo no.'

I waited for him continue, but he didn't. The waitress brought his order and he lifted the lid off the pot and stirred his tea.

'No,' he smiled, 'Never been a bridegroom – plenty of times the best man though.'

'Sounds a bit like "Always the bridesmaid and never the bride".'

'Mmm,' he continued stirring the tea.

'Oh, come on.'

'Come on what?'

'I can tell by that smile. You must have a wedding story.'

'Funny, you should say that; I was told a strange tale about a bridegroom and, he smiled and said,

"Colin's Buttonhole ...

Colin was pleased with his reflection. The mirror on Mother's wardrobe door, though speckled with age, only cut off his legs from below the knee. He glanced down and smiled at his polished black shoes – and the two exact bows of the laces. Perfection.

He held the yellow carnation to his nose, sniffed, then frowned. No smell. He pushed the flower's silver foiled stem into his lapel buttonhole, lifting his chin away from the tickling fern. He turned to check the time on the bedside clock. Five minutes, then his best man – Uncle Len's stepson Wayne – would be here.

Colin closed his eyes and tried to shut out the vision of Wayne. He glanced at his reflection again and tutted. The carnation had fallen out. He looked down but couldn't see it. He stooped and felt under the wardrobe. Not there. Carefully pinching the creases of his pinstriped trousers he knelt, lifted the side of the bedspread and peered into the gloom. He flapped a palm across the carpet. Nothing except fluff. He stood up grunting with exertion and pulled down his cuffs. He tutted again at his reflection when he saw that his cravat had become undone. One end of the gold silk had strayed across his lapel. He tried to flick it down, not wanting to crease the material, but it seemed snagged. As he tugged, the cravat unwound from his neck and disappeared. He spun round thinking the cravat had fallen on the floor behind him, but it wasn't there. He half turned and looked in the mirror hoping to see it dangling down his back. It wasn't. He stepped out onto the landing. 'Wayne? Are you there, messing about?' There was no reply. Colin opened the bathroom door. Empty. He went into his bedroom. No one. He pushed at the junk room door; it only opened a couple of inches. Colin knew no one could get in there. Back in Mother's room, he walked round to the far side of the double bed and lifted the bedspread. Nothing but fluff.

If Wayne had been upstairs or even downstairs, he would have heard Colin's squeal of panic when the bridegroom stood again in front of Mother's wardrobe mirror. Colin had his hand to his throat; his fingers digging into the flesh trying to find the white starched collar that minutes before had been round his neck. Colin ran back out onto the landing and started down the stairs; he missed the last two treads, but grabbed the newel post and kept his balance. He clung to the varnished wood and watched the front door, willing the bell to ring.

'Wayne! Wayne!' his voice was a choke. He listened. Silence. He stumbled across the hall and peered through the pebbled glass of the front door; he saw the distorted path and gate. The hedge wobbled as he pressed his face closer to the pane. There was no sign of Wayne or the black limousine. He went into the living room and stared out of the bay window onto the empty street.

Colin lifted his wrist to look as his watch. He fell against the china cabinet with a scream. His white shirt cuffs had gone – both of them. He pushed one hand up the sleeve of his jacket, then the other. He had no shirtsleeves. He slapped his hands onto his chest; first feeling the rough brocade of his waistcoat then … then … his fingers touched the hairs on his chest. He jumped up and ran to the fireplace. The oval mirror showed the face of a middle-aged man with thinning hair and over-large ears. Colin gripped the edge of the mantelpiece, stepped onto the fender and his shoulders came into view. As he looked, his shirt billowed out from behind his jacket collar, wafted near his head like an half developed spectre and then squeeze through his lapel buttonhole. Colin clutched at the cotton, but it slipped through his fingers. He watched himself looking at the disappearing material. Then he dropped his eyes, stared at his bare neck and the bare V of his chest. He saw his waistcoat; his golden waistcoat begin to ride up towards his neck – he felt the buckles undo and ping against his spine and ...no ... the satin fabric slithered over his shoulder and vanished into his lapel buttonhole like a snake into its nest.

Colin fell from the fender onto his knees. He began to cry; dry little sobs like coughs. He crouched into a ball on the hearthrug. His sobs caught his breath and he gulped for air. Suddenly he was aware his trousers felt tight: too tight. He knelt upright as he had on the altar steps with his Rita at their rehearsal two days ago. His stomach hurt. His bum, his thighs. He stood up and ... rip ... frayed lengths of serge fell from his body. He pulled at his jacket; dragged it off, leaving the sleeves inside out and threw it across the room. It slithered over the parquet floor; the leather pouffe stopped its journey. It lay like a drunk. Colin couldn't take his eyes off the jacket; he stared at the lapel buttonhole. The slit, neatly bound in black silk, opened and greedily sucked in what had been his trousers. Colin thought: this isn't happening. This is ... nerves

... it's panic. It's wedding ... wedding. He shouted out:

'Wayne. Where are you?' Even Wayne's tattooed head and pierced eyebrow would be welcome.

His shoes, polished to perfection last evening, came off in a flick. He noticed the laces didn't untie, but stayed as prissy bows. His grey woollen socks followed and danced themselves into the shoes. The shoes then clattered over to the jacket and the buttonhole opened its silky lips wide and swallowed them whole. Colin squeezed his arms over his bare chest and shook.

Then he had a horrible thought and clutched the waistband of his underpants. It was no use. They dropped to his ankles and with a yelp Colin jumped away from them. He watched as the buttonhole first pursed its black lips, then inhaled. His M&S pale blue Y-fronts were gone. Colin perched on the arm of a chair. He told himself none of this was happening. In a moment there would be a ring on the bell and Wayne - where the hell had the fool got to? - would be there.

Colin looked round the room for something to cover himself. He pulled at the lace chair-back and wrapped it like a loincloth round his hips. He had to get out of the room - but to do so he had to get past the jacket. He inched towards the door. One leap, he told himself.

One leap and he'd be out of the room, up the stairs and locked in the bathroom. Bugger Wayne. Bugger the Wedding.

It was as Colin leapt – and the chair-back slipped from his body that the jacket rose. It floated up from the floor, its white lining arms stretching out. It reached forward and crushed Colin to itself. The last thing Colin saw was a perfectly tailored lapel buttonhole before it opened into a black chasm and Colin was no more.

***

Mother was not pleased that Wayne had broken the lock of the front door. Mother, Uncle Len and Doris, his second wife; Rita of course, and her two cousins had eventually been persuaded by Wayne to return home and help search for Colin. (The vicar had been none too pleased either). The jacket and the lace chair-back on the floor were a complete mystery. Wayne having hunted around upstairs added to the mystery when he came downstairs with the yellow carnation.

'Look,' he said, 'This is all I can find. Colin's buttonhole.' "

My cappuccino was getting cold. I drank it quickly and said, 'I don't believe a word.'

He smiled and said, 'Don't you?'

*

7th Story

  I took a sip of my cappuccino. As he sat down, the waitress brought him his tea.
  I said, 'Why have we got these on the table?' I held up a place mat, 'Don't like them, do you?'
  He shook his head.
  'I heard that Dominic is away for a month or two; his cousin is running the coffee shop.'
  He looked at his place mat. 'Edinburgh Castle'.
  I took another sip, 'Well, I'm glad the coffee is still just as I like it.'
  I moved my place mat away, 'Tower of London. Very 1970s.'
  He didn't answer; he finished his tea; and was pouring out a second cup then said, 'My cousin has a set of place mats; they were a present – a special present ...' he paused,
  ... and?' I prompted.
  He smiled and said:

    "Poor Belinda ...

Belinda answered her phone.

'Sonia! I don't believe it. How wonderful! How did you get my number?

'With great difficulty, Belinda, I can assure you.'

'It's lovely, lovely to hear from you.'

'How are you? Nobody has heard a word from you.'

'Well … Arthur …'

'Never mind about him,' interrupted Sonia, 'but I hear he's making a name for himself in the world of finance.'

'I know, he …

'Saw him on TV the other night.'

'Yes and of course the children …'

'And never mind about them,'

Belinda laughed, 'I have to mind about them.'

'Not all the time surely,' Sonia sounded a bit cross, 'Haven't you got *au pairs* and nannies and things.'

'Yes, but Arthur likes me …'

There was a strange noise on the phone. Belinda said, 'Are you growling Sonia?'

'Yes I am. Never mind what Arthur likes. What would you like?'

'Oh, I don't know.'

'A trip up to London? Lunch? Art Gallery?'

'Be wonderful, but … I don't know.'

Sonia said, 'Leave it with me,' and rang off.

***

Belinda had been an artist; a successful one. She had obtained several commissions as soon as she had left Art School and her exhibitions were always a triumph. She was pretty; had big greeny/blue eyes and despite her auburn hair, a sweet nature. By her early thirties she had an elegant apartment in that part of London that was not a surprise to those in the know. Once a year she would pack up her painting paraphernalia and travel by train, never by plane, to Spain, Italy, Greece, Turkey, set up her easel in city squares; along village lanes; by rivers; in the shade of mountains; next to the sea. Back home another exhibition – well attended, well reviewed and sold out.

It was when she was in Villaneuva de Pedro a few miles from Cordoba that she met Arthur. She was sitting in a lane trying to get the shade of blue she needed for the morning Spanish sky when he cycled past. Well, he didn't cycle past, his handlebar caught the canvas and knocked the easel over. He was very apologetic; helped Belinda set up her work again and offered her some tea from his flask. She thought the tea was vile – it being made with long life milk, but smiled her thanks. She was going to be in the village of Villaneuva de Pedro for a while   –   she wanted to paint its church and two days later Arthur cycled up, stopped and offered her a square of chocolate. She took it quickly as it was melting, then sucked her fingers clean. He stood behind her, never making any comment about her work, but told her he was an accountant with a London firm. Belinda had heard of the company, in fact they had dealt with some of her financial problems.

'What a coincidence,' she said squeezing the ultramarine onto the palette.

He came along again the next day only stopping to ask where she was going next. 'Seville,' she said. Arthur said he might see her there. She nodded and when she turned round he had cycled away.

She had packed away her work for the day and as she stepped from behind one of the horse and carriages opposite the La Giralda Arthur pulled up beside her. From then on he always seemed to be wherever she set up her easel. Not stalking she told herself, just friendly. He never showed any interest in her paintings. He talked about figures and balances, about meetings and deadlines, but for all that Belinda liked him. He didn't smile very much, but he was ... what was the word she was looking for? Nice? If he didn't talk about "his sums" as Belinda called them, he told her about his cycle trips around Spain.

Every year a different region. Galicia, Extremadura, Murcia and this year Andalusia.

When back in London, it seemed a natural for them to meet up first for coffee, then it was lunch, then dinner and finally Arthur stayed over in the elegant apartment. The following year they married. Belinda was grateful for a sound, down to earth person to take care of all those humdrum parts of her life.

'Not humdrum at all,' argued Arthur.

The babies came along. Little Arthur arrived the day after their first wedding anniversary; Alfie the following year; with the birth of the third boy, Belinda forestalled Arthur,

'I'd like James.'

'Fine. Alexander James.'

With the arrival of twins Agnes and Augusta, Belinda said, 'Enough.'

Belinda loved her children; she was always happy with them and they were happy with her. If there was anything wrong with her life it was her art, or rather the lack of it. In their grand house in Sussex a room could easily have been used as a studio, but Arthur thought it unnecessary. 'You've got the children,' he said.

'They'll grow up and not need me,' she pointed out.

'But it's a waste of time,' argued Arthur.

How do I find an answer to that thought Belinda. It was a few weeks after the twins third birthday when Sonia had rung.

Sonia arranged everything.

'Next Tuesday I will collect you at 10 o'clock sharp; be ready. We stop for coffee; then a little shopping at Fortnum & Mason. Lunch – which is a going to be a surprise – all to be an early birthday present for you – and then onto the N G for …'

'Not the Van Gogh exhibition? interrupted Belinda.

'Yes,' crooned Sonia.

'I thought it was finished.'

'Only a few days left.'

'All sounds heavenly. Thank you; thank you. You are a wonderful friend, Sonia.'

'Think nothing of it,'

'Sunflowers! The sunflowers! those yellows: honey, gold, saffron …'

'It will be heavenly,' agreed Sonia,' and I have to say this, there will be no probs driving or parking in central London,' she paused, 'I have friends, of friends.'

'Oh?'

'Say nothing to that husband of yours,' Sonia laughed, 'Keep it under your artist's beret.'

'Next Tuesday? I intended working from home that day,' said Arthur.

'Querina will be here, and Nanny. I'm sure not to be that late home.'

'Mmm.' Arthur poured himself a glass of Pinot Noir and went into his study.

Belinda was ready and waiting when she heard the tooting of the Aston Martin. She kissed the children goodbye, promised presents and put her head round the study door.

'Arthur, I'm going now.'

He looked up from the laptop and stared at her, 'Going where?'

'Don't tease Arthur. National Gallery. Van Gogh. Sonia. Won't be late home. Promise.'

The coffee bar was very modern and the coffee very strong. The presents from Fortnum & Mason were very expensive and the lunch was very, as Belinda said, out of this world. Belinda stood at the top of the National Gallery steps and watched students and tourists chattering and scattering across the Square; she followed a red queue of buses circling past the Nelson's Column before splitting away into different directions; showers of water from the fountains were being tossed away by the breeze. The noise; the smell; the colours; the movement wrapped around her – the home in Sussex with its glossy kitchen worktops; carpets deep and silent, antique furniture polished to a heavy dullness were floating away on another planet.

'Okay,' said Sonia looking at the tickets, 'We are in perfect time for our slot.'

They walked through the entrance and were queuing to have their bags checked by security when Belinda's mobile rang. She stepped out of the queue.

'Arthur? Hello. Anything wrong?'

She listened to him.

'Are you sure? What does Nanny say?'

She listened some more.

'All right Arthur. I'll tell Sonia.'

Arthur was still talking.

'Yes. Yes. Arthur. As soon as I can.'

Sonia had been watching.

'Well?'

'It's Agnes. She's had a little choking fit. Arthur says ...'

'Is she all right?'

'Yes. Yes. Now she is, but Arthur wants her checked at A & E.'

Sonia flicked the tickets across Belinda's hand. 'Well, he'd better take her.'

'Oh, no Sonia. I must take her. I must get home. Get a taxi.'

Belinda looked round as though she expected one to be parked next to her.

'Belinda, you just can't go now. Half an hour – that's all; and you will have seen it.'

'Don't be silly, Sonia. I'm sorry, but I must leave now.'

'Fine. Fine. We'll go.'

Belinda and Sonia were silent with each on the way back to Sussex. As Sonia parked in the drive Belinda did say, 'Sonia I'm sorry.'

'No Belinda. I'm the one that's sorry. I wanted the *Sunflowers* to be for you; that was what the day was all about.' "

I looked at him and said, 'Poor Belinda - and she never got to see Van Gogh's *Sunflowers*?

He put down his empty cup.

'Oh, yes she did. I went to have supper with them – and there were the *Sunflowers*. Half a dozen of them'

I frowned at him, 'How?'

'On a set of place mats. Arthur bought them; for her birthday.'

'Poor Belinda,' I said.

*

8th Story

I looked at the chocolate sprinkles on the froth of my cappuccino. What on earth was it supposed to be? I twisted the cup around trying to make sense of the shape.

'Hello. You look perplexed.'

'Hi.' I said, 'Are you going to join me?'

'Of course.' He sat down. 'Anything the matter?'

I laughed, 'No, just trying to make out this shape.'

'It's like looking at clouds. First you see one thing, then it changes into another.'

'Well,' I said, 'This looks like a lizard. Ugh.'

He smiled a thank you to the waitress as she served his tea.

I started to sip my cappuccino.

'Tastes good?' he asked.

'Yes; as always.'

'There,' he said, 'Never judge by appearances.'

'But lizards are lizards,' I argued.'

'You've reminded me ....'

'Of a story,' I interrupted.

He poured out his tea, smiled and said :

"Never Judge By Appearances ...

'Once upon a time,' mused Toucan.

'Mmm?' Lizard wasn't interested. He lifted his face to the sun.

'This is a story about Jaguar. Listen – you'll like it,'

Lizard sighed.

Toucan began again: 'Once upon a time Jaguar was feeling particularly miserable – do you know why?'

'No.'

'Hunger.'

'Hunger? A Jaguar hungry?' Lizard stretched and relaxed his back legs.

'Yes. Jaguar was hungry; he hadn't eaten for days. He just didn't seem to be able to catch anything. He spent hours crouched by the rock pool watching fish dart this way and that, but just as he was about to scoop one, it would flick away from his claws. He even tried the old dangling his tail in the water ruse; swishing it around to entice them near the surface, but no luck.

'When he wasn't at the pool, he padded through the forest, eyes ever sharp, ears pricked, but even as he slinked along, not making a sound through the undergrowth, he was unable to surprise a wild pig or even a capybara.

'He climbed trees and sprawled on overhanging branches to watch and wait for something tasty to scurry unconcerned out from its den because he knew, like a slash from a sword, he could be onto the creature but ...'

'Nothing?' said a now interested Lizard.

'Nothing. He never saw a thing. It was, I said, a miserable time for Jaguar. He considered himself so superior to other animals: a creature of magnificence.

'A god,' suggested Lizard.

'True,' conceded Toucan. 'Lord of the Earth ...'

'With supernatural powers,' interrupted Lizard.

'Lord of the Earth,' Toucan's beak closed with a particularly loud crack.

Lizard grinned: 'And there he was with belly ache.'

Toucan fixed an eye on Lizard and continued: 'Jaguar considered himself superior to other animals. Meanwhile ...'

'Meanwhile what?'

'This story has to have a "Meanwhile" as I am now going to take you to another part of the forest.'

Toucan waited. In the distance, the monkeys' noisy prattling grew louder, then faded as a danger passed.

'Meanwhile ... Two-toed Sloth was tired. For the past week he had been travelling along a branch. Hanging upside down, he'd used his long arms to inch forward, his claws managing to hook and drag at the leaves and ferns. Two-toed frequently stopped to ponder and chew. He was weary and soon he'd have the chore of leaving the branch for the ground, but not yet. As the day crept on, his gradual journey slowed and very nearly ceased. Then the loden gloom surrounded him: his large eyes closed and he nestled his snub nose into his fur and his body stopped moving.'

Toucan paused.

Turning round for his back to feel the sun Lizard said: 'So? Is that it?'

Toucan waited for Lizard to stop fidgeting.

'Of course not. In the sunless undergrowth of the forest, algae thrives and spreads. It grows on the twigs, trunks, branches of the trees. The dankness of the under wood had hung about Two-toed Sloth for so long that even his drab brown hair was tinged with green vegetation.'

Lizard shivered.

'So,' continued Toucan.' Picture the scene. A silent, shaded forest. A sleeping Two-toed Sloth. When who should come prowling, but Jaguar.'

'Bye, bye Two-toed,' sniggered Lizard.

'With each soft step, the chains of black rosettes dappled across his rich golden fur, then Jaguar paused, his whiskers trembled. Every sense was acute. He waited. Nothing moved. He noiselessly climbed onto a log, then a low bough of a tree. He stretched up to a higher branch and tight-roped walked across, carefully stepping over Two-toed Sloth that, for all the world, looked like a bunch of evergreen leaves. When Jaguar reached the end of the branch he paused, sniffed the damp air, turned and looked again along the branch. He retraced his steps; as he got to the hanging foliage he stopped, his front paw hovering over Two-toed Sloth. He lowered his head, his amber eyes absorbing the mossy, leafy clump, then the branch shook as his angry tail thrashed from side to side. Jaguar balanced for a moment on the swaying branch, jumped back down onto the log and sneaked away into deeper undergrowth and continued to hunt.'

'And Two-toed Sloth?' asked Lizard.

'He opened his eyes, eventually, then eventually, closed then again.'

'Wow,' said Lizard. 'That was a good story.'

'So remember Friend.' Toucan stretched his aching spine. 'Never judge by appearances.'
As he spoke that last word, his beak snapped and Lizard was swallowed whole. "

I laughed, picked up my spoon and swilled the froth around, 'And that's the end of my lizard.'

*

9th Story

The waitress put down my cappuccino. I noticed there were no tongs in the sugar bowl. I stood up to go to get some and bumped into him.

'Sorry.'

'No my fault,' he smiled.

'I need the tongs, I said.

He reached over and asked for them from the next table.

As his tea was being served he said, 'Does anyone play that?'

I looked to where he was pointing.

'The piano? No. Dominic painted it with the lid closed, and now it won't open. I think the emerald green was the only paint he could find.'

'That's a shame.'

'What the colour?'

'No,' he laughed, 'That the lid's stuck.'

'Do you play?'

'Not the piano – clarinet.'

'Love that instrument. Do you play with a group or … ?' I suddenly thought I was as asking too many questions.

'Now, just for my own amusement.'

I drank a little of my coffee, and as I put down the cup realised I had given myself a frothy moustache.

'Though I am fond of the piano,' he continued, pouring out his tea, 'Been to some wonderful concerts; heard some great pianists over the years. Once saw Askenazy.'

'No? Really. Lucky you. My Dad bought me one of his LPs. LP! My, that's going back a few years.'

I found a tissue in my cardigan pocket and dabbed at my lips – didn't want to end up with smearing lipstick all over my face.

'I know of a strange tale about a pianist.'

'Oh?'

I rested my elbows on the table. 'Tell me … please.'

He took a sip of tea smiled and said,

"Identity Crisis …

Steffan didn't set out to be a killer. It just happened. He often thought, during the following months after the "incident" - as he always referred to it in his mind - that had the day started differently, it would have ended differently. They had breakfasted in bed. He had padded down when they heard the newspaper boy's bicycle skim the gravel. Back in the bedroom he had tossed the newspaper over to her and gone into the bathroom. That one review; some Aussie ignoramus who knew nothing of music; nothing of ... She was leaning back on the pillows, laughing and flapping the paper like a fan, said: 'Darling, darling, let m-e-e-e read it to y-o-o-o.'

He tried to tug the newspaper from her, but she wouldn't let go. Why hadn't she just let go ... then everything would have been different.

***

The wide gates had been opened and Roger Mace drove up to the front door. He knew he should have left his car outside the double garage, but liked the sound of the gravel spinning from under his tyres. He took his case from the passenger seat and ran up the porch steps. The door was ajar and as he pushed it wide the late afternoon sun stretched across the polished wood floor. Roger knew he was expected so went straight along the hall into the drawing room and across to the baby grand. After he had been working for about ten minutes, he went out into the hall and listened: *The Brandenburg Concerto* was echoing from the conservatory. Roger shrugged – one of the old fool's favourite CDs – and returned to the drawing room.

'What are doing?'

Roger spun round. 'I thought you were in the conservatory.'

'Obviously. Now I ask you again – what are you doing?'

Roger glanced at the figurine he was holding, then smirked, 'Just taking a little extra payment. A bonus shall we say?'

'Put it back.'

'Now now Mr Bergman you can't give me orders.'

'Roger, I can and I will. Please put that figurine back in the cabinet and whether you have finished tuning my piano or not, leave my house.'

Roger bent down and put the figurine in his case and snapped it shut. Bergman rushed forward to grab the case, but Roger pushed him away and started across the room. Bergman overtook him and barred his way.

'Shift.' Roger's voice was soft.

'I will call the police.'

'Shift I said,'

Roger tried to pull him away from the door; Bergman lunged at him, but Roger side stepped and Bergman, losing his balance, fell. He stayed on the floor for a moment, then tried to sit up, but dropped down holding on to his arm. Roger thought his breathing sounded horrible.

'Get up do.'

He turned and lifted down two silver candlesticks from the mantelpiece and put them in his case. He squatted beside the inert man and shook his shoulder. His breathing seemed quieter.

'For God's sake, you're not that hurt.'

Roger watched Bergman for a moment then dragging him away from the door, propped him against the wall. He slipped out of the drawing room, crossed the hall, fastened the catch on the front door and took the stairs two at a time. On the landing all the doors were shut. Roger opened one; closed it again – a lumber room. He opened the door opposite and stepped over the thick carpet to a tall-boy standing next to the bed. The top drawer slid open silently. Roger pushed aside some balled socks and found a box; he lifted the lid; the Rolex watch sat expensively on the black velvet. Roger pulled the watch over his fist and shook down his cuff. Neatly stacked vests and pants were in the second drawer. Roger tried the third. Between the folds of a Fair Isle knitted sweater was a bundle of rolled notes. As Roger flicked the corners, the elastic band pinged off and £50 notes fluttered on to the sweater; Roger scrabbled them together, pushed the drawer shut with his hip and ran down the stairs.

Bergman was still against the wall; Roger pushed his foot into the man's thigh.

'Whassup? C'mon.'

Roger stooped and nudged the man's jaw, 'Get up. D'yer hear?'

He felt the side of Bergman's neck, then realised that the man wouldn't be hearing anything ever again. He crossed to the sofa and flopped down.

God! What a mess! He glanced at Bergman. Call an ambulance? He looked at his wrist; at the two watches. He wound the Rolex and, checking against his Filling Station £5 bargain, turned the hands to the correct time. How much time had passed? Sudden death equals police. He'd watched enough TV dramas to know all about time of death et cetera. It looked like an ordinary heart attack.

'Where were you Mr Mace?'

'I was outside, Officer, looking for something in my car.'

'What exactly happened Mr Mace?'

'I don't know …'

'Why Mr Mace didn't you …?'

'I didn't realise.'

'When Mr Mace …?'

Roger took out his mobile phone, jabbed at the "9" and again, was about to do it for the third time, then paused:

'Did you move the body Mr Mace?'

'Well, I …'

'Why did you move the body Mr Mace?'

'Well, I …?'

Roger cancelled the call and dropped the mobile by his feet.

'What shall I do Mr Steffan Bergman? What shall I do?'

Roger pondered his life; a one-bedroom flat over a pet shop; a fifteen-year old car that, he was sure, was not going to pass its next MOT. Women. There had been a few, but now the only ones he met at the pub had too much baggage, too much flab, too much … he just couldn't be bothered. He was his own boss true, but always the constant worry of new contracts. He spent most of his working days in grand, luxurious houses like this – enough to irritate any ordinary person; the owner's casual acceptance of wealth and power and privilege … while he … while his mother … had scrimped and saved for his lessons with old Ma Bartlett …

The figurine and the candlesticks were back on display. The watch was still on his wrist and the money in his wallet He played the answer phone, but there weren't any messages; in the study he leafed through the dead man's diary, there was nothing apart from an appointment for a dental check-up booked for the following week. Roger sat at Bergman's desk and read through all the paperwork that was there. He was amazed; Bergman had no computer; ipad, laptop so it was like going through his mother's financial affairs twenty years ago. Utility bills were in date order and filed in ring binders. He only seemed to have one current account – the statements again all in chronological order; the balance showing £186,439:67. There were direct debits set up for all the bills and Roger noticed £500 cash was always withdrawn on the 2nd of every month, the day after £5,600:00 was credited to the account. The bank card was in an envelope and Roger tutted, "Oh, dear Mr Bergman, you were a Silly Billy," when he noticed four digits written on the envelope. Roger found no record of any savings accounts, shares, letters from stock brokers or documents relating to insurance. He let the swivel chair turn him away from the desk. It all seemed good … too good … to be true?

An hour later and he had made a decision. He had put the body in the boot of his car, and the car was in the garage. He made several calls on his mobile cancelling future work. He spoke to his landlord, the owner of the pet shop and told him he had an important commitment in Scotland and would be away for two or three months, but not to worry about the rent. He phoned his local to say he couldn't play in Friday's dart match as his sister had been taken ill and he was off to Yorkshire. He cancelled the check-up at the dentist, then sat at the piano and played a selection from *The Mikado,* and Chopin's *Minute Waltz.*

In the kitchen, he cut slices from a crusty loaf, found butter and cheese and made a sandwich. There was no beer in the frig – just several bottles of white wine. At midnight he made another sandwich; this time ham. He dozed on the sofa, but during the early hours went upstairs and, in another bedroom, fell asleep on a narrow single bed.

The next day Roger stayed in the house. He wanted to discover Bergman's routine, but nothing untoward seemed to happen. In the morning while he was waiting for the toast and trying to fathom the workings of the coffee machine he heard footsteps on the drive. The kitchen was at the side of the house, but Roger pulled at the Venetian blind cord and closed the slats. A minute later the footsteps receded and Roger, going into the hall, saw a postcard in the wire box attached to the front door. The postcard had a view of a beach in the Algarve and the message read: *"Just keeping in touch – Erik."*

In the dining room was a sideboard; again Roger suddenly thought of his mother and her small, cramped home. The two doors of the sideboard were locked and Roger pulled so hard that one of the metal knobs came away in his hand; he felt frustrated at this first obstacle; he fetched a kitchen knife and dug into the side of the door to prise it open. Bundles of sheet music fell onto the floor. He reached inside and pulled out the box files; he counted – there were eight. He carried them over to the dining table and sat down.

Three boxes contained dozens of letters from a Gabriela. Bergman and she had obviously been lovers. She had written two, three, sometimes four times a weeks to where he was performing in cities all over the world. Some of the letters seemed to have overtaken earlier ones that he hadn't received for she was constantly demanding why he hadn't replied. Roger surmised that she was married and that she was more keen for the affair to continue than he.

The other boxes were full of press cuttings and reviews. Bergman had been a successful concert pianist – good looking, charming, affable; the darling of middle aged, middle-class women in Europe, America, Australia. One of the last reviews was dated two years ago. Roger read it through twice; he chortled. It was not a good review; it was a stinker.

He heard the grandfather clock strike four. He went into kitchen and opened a tin of tomato soup, heated it in a saucepan, and leaning against the cooker, drank it from the saucepan. Then he made a decision. Tin of soup! What was he doing pigging it like this? In the utility room was a freezer. Roger found two large trout and laid them out to de-frost. Also in the freezer was a raspberry gateau; he put that on a plate.

The following day it rained; heavy and constant. Roger re-read all the press cuttings and reviews; picked out a few tunes on the piano. He played some CDs; when he had seen *The Brandenburg Concerto* still in the machine he'd thrown it in the kitchen pedal-bin.

That evening Roger made another decision. It was after midnight when he felt satisfied with his work. The bathroom mirror reflected, not a sandy haired, discontented piano tuner in cheap shirt, shiny off-the-peg trousers, but a bald, slightly stooped man, dressed in expensive jumper, slacks and loafers. Roger knew good luck was on his side as rummaging through the dead man's wardrobe, shirts, trousers, shoes all fitted with perfection; his satisfaction compounded with the quality of the clothes and designer labels.

On the third morning Roger explored the garden; the driveway encircled a lawn that ran from the house to the front lane. A row of leylandii blocked anyone seeing the house from the lane. Wide patches of grass grew by each side of the house; at the rear Roger thought it was more like a paddock than a back garden; at the far boundary another row of leylandii hid marsh land. A few mildewed rose bushes grew next to the fences each side of the house. Roger found a metal garden chair, steadied it against one fence and climbed up. For as far as he could see was scrub land; then in the distance, the flyover of the by-pass. He took the chair over to the other fence. Here was a tangle of brambles, diseased trees and weeds. Roger knew the house was isolated; he always thought about that when he drove to it from the village. He put the chair in the middle of the grass and sat down. It all looked good ... so far. Suddenly Roger's heart gave a leap. All this grass! It must have been mowed a while back; it was now quite long; the edges ragged. Bergman might have a gardener. He might call tomorrow; today; any minute. Roger stumbled back into the house. At the sink he held his head under the tap and gulped at the water. He went into the study and found the diary. He knew he had already scanned the first page; but still he read it again: *"Health Centre"* followed by a local number, *"Optician"* again with a local number, *"Erik"* with an international dialling code and number. Nothing else. Roger turned the pages forward and back then dropped the diary on the desk.

He hurried out of the house, past the garage with his car. He opened the door of the second garage. By the side of the BMW was a lawn mower; a sit-on poncy affair; so big it was known as a lawn tractor. His racing heart slowed.

The next day he went out in the BMW. He drove over thirty miles and found a gastro pub, chose extravagantly from the menu, but only had half a pint of larger. On the way home he shopped, for the sake of it, at a supermarket. The following day he drove in the opposite direction and stopped at a country club and had a three course lunch; he then went on to a large town in the next county and bought some CDs. He wanted to get some decent up-to-date music equipment, but hesitated. Stores weren't always keen to take cash. He still had enough money from the bundle he had found, but was reluctant at using the card, but knew he would have to in time.

For the next few evenings he just went out and drove along country lanes. He knew, though he couldn't say it to himself, what he was looking for. He had to get rid of the body. One evening he drove to the coast, parked at a picnic spot near the cliffs and wandered around. He suddenly felt conspicuous. A young couple he passed as he was returning to the car turned and watched him; afterwards he thought they had been interested in the BMW. It was noticeable; cherry red and the latest registration. Perhaps he should use his own car. No. He couldn't. But he would have to for "that journey." Rather than keep driving around he bought an ordnance survey map. He thought he had found a good spot – a river some 70 miles away, but … always a "but" …

He made himself forget about the body. For nearly three weeks, he lounged around; played the piano – it was a beautiful instrument. He stocked up on beer; he ate well. He even slept in the double bed after he had stripped and changed the bedding. Every morning he put on different clothes; tossed what he had worn the day before in the lumber room. He did use the card to withdraw money at ATMs – every time a different location, and eventually used it to buy a music centre. He longed to have a laptop, computer, anything; regretted not having his ipad with him, but knew he had to be wary. He once thought about driving back to the flat and collecting it, but knew the BMW parked outside the pet shop, even at night, was a crazy idea. And he kept looking at the grass. Every day it was getting higher and more untidy. He wanted everything to remain the same, so knew he'd have to make the effort and mow it before long. But first … first … the body.

He woke one morning again to heavy rain. Today, he thought. It's going to be today. He cooked himself a full English. He didn't make a too bad a job of the fried bread; not as good as his mother used to make, but then she stopped cooking it for him when she read how unhealthy it was. Later, he spread the map on the study floor, slid his fingers from edge to edge; top to bottom. Then found the place.

His heart was hammering and he felt sweat all over his body as he opened the door. He sniffed hard; just the usual dank garage smell. He threw the rucksack on the passenger's seat, got in and turned the ignition; started first time. He ran his palms across his tee shirt ... and remembered. He had filled up on the by-pass that day, just before getting to the house. He kissed the air. He noticed the difference in driving his car after the BMW, but he wasn't being noticed; that was important.

By the middle of the morning, the rain had stopped, though they day remained dull and murky. It was dusk when he reached the place; it had been a long drive; the petrol gauge showed that the tank was nearly empty, but none of that mattered now. The car tyres cracked over loose stones; the noise seemed too loud, but he hadn't seen another vehicle in the last hour. He parked and dropped down the dash; found two pencils and an opened packet of chewing gum; in the door ledge an empty water bottle. He stuffed all of it into the rucksack; then with a cloth rubbed at the steering wheel, gears, hand brake, the dashboard; everywhere. He took the rucksack and climbed out of the car; walked round it and again rubbed at every surface he imagined he might have touched. He stood by the boot.

Everywhere was grey. The sky, the track; he looked down – the water. He unlocked the boot and, as he pushed it up, gagged. He held the cloth to his mouth and reached in for his anorak. It was wedged under the hip; he hanked at the hood; it came away and the body moved; to him, it seemed into a more comfortable position. He slammed the boot and scrubbed at the paintwork. Prising off the registration plates was easy; he smirked to himself: only rust had kept them on. He stamped, twisted, bent them, then stood on the edge of the pit, stretched back his arm and threw. He knew he wasn't much of an athlete, but watching the metal arc was pleased how long it took before he heard the *spwish* when they hit the water. He leaned his back against the boot and pushed; the tyres skidded on the gravel. It took longer than he thought. He turned, was going to put his palms on the car, then remembered and continued leaning against the boot, walking backwards. He stopped when he felt the front wheels tip forward; took a moment to catch his breath, then one more push and the weight was gone and he fell backwards onto the stones. He crawled to edge and looked down. The car was bouncing, twisting, then it stopped. To him it seemed forever, but then it began rolling again and he saw the water move, open up then close over the roof of the car.

It took three days to get back. The first night, he slept in an animal shelter ten miles from the gravel pit. As soon as he saw the car disappear he had grabbed the rucksack and set off. He hiked the next day; once thumbing a lift, but the truck driver, bored, asked too many questions. That night he stayed in a pub; the busy landlord ignored him. The following night he chose a bed and breakfast in a quiet village. As he was going to bed thought perhaps it hadn't been a good idea. This was a small place with an inquisitive woman. The following morning he walked to the nearby town and caught a train to within twenty miles of home. It was late evening when he left the train, and he chanced the final trek back through the night. It was just getting light when he walked through the gates; he opened the front door, dropped the rucksack and pulled off all his clothes. With his eyes closed stood under the hot water until he felt himself rock against the tiles. He stepped out of the shower, wrapped himself in a towel, and fell onto the bed. It was evening when he woke; he was hungry and cooked himself another fry-up.

In the morning he looked from the bedroom window at the grass, but didn't go into the garden. He played the piano; selections from *My Fair Lady* and *Oklahoma*. His fingers fluttered over the keys again and again. After the fifth time he played *I'm Getting Married in the Morning* he crashed the lid closed and looked round the drawing room; at the heavy draped curtains, the antique rugs; the cabinet full of valuable porcelain. I could have had all this, he told himself. I was good. I am good. I never had the chance, not like … not like … Well, I've got it now, haven't I?

He enjoyed cutting the grass; up and down, making lanes; keeping as straight as possible. Perched on the mower – there was nothing to it. Should anyone manage to peer through the conifers and see him – it would be Mr Bergman tidying up his garden. The next day he wanted another physical job; pruning the roses wasn't for him- anyway they looked passed saving. By the side of the garage he found a brazier. A bonfire! That's it; he'd have a bonfire. He brought out of the house armfuls of music magazines; shredded them. On a shelf in the garage was a box of matches; he smiled; everything he needed. The paper burned quickly; the garage doors were open and he saw the lawn mower; grass cuttings. He emptied them onto the blaze and they immediately damped down the flames. The fire was nearly out. He ran back into the house. Hunted in kitchen cupboards, looked in the utility room. He thought about all the bills and bank statements, but decided against them. The press cuttings! He carried out three of the boxes and tipped the contents into the brazier; thick smoke made his eyes water. A garden fork hung on the garage wall and he used it to stir the press cuttings. He watched the edge of a blackened paper turn to yellow, gold and then the flames shot up. He fetched the other two boxes and emptied them onto the fire. He wondered if Bergman would have ever burnt them. Then he thought of the letters. It was as he was carrying the boxes across the hall he heard first little pops; then crack; one, two, three, then the *whoosh*. He stepped out on to the porch and saw the flames stretching across the open garage doors. Dropping the boxes he ran towards the brazier, the explosion threw him backwards. He stumbled up; the fire was spreading inside the garage; there was another splitting crack and another explosion. Flames now covered the lawn mower and were riding up the side of the BMW; there was another loud crack; the fire spread out of the side window. He stood there. What to do? What the hell to do? He became aware of a car stopping by the gates. Someone was calling. Then he saw a truck. Two men were rattling the gates. Still he stood there. He heard words – "Fire Brigade" – "Injured" – "Help". He turned away and ran round the side of the house to the back garden. He dropped down onto the neat lawn. What to do? He didn't know if it was five minutes later or fifty minutes, when he heard the siren. He opened the back door, went through the kitchen and up to the bedroom and locked the door. From the window he watched the gates being wrenched open, the fire engine, the men, the hoses, the busyness. The last curls of smoke. The roof of the garage had gone; the walls black. Two firemen went into the garage; one came out and spoke to the group. There were voices in the hall, footsteps on the stairs. No one came to the bedroom door. He sat on the edge of the bed. The noise of more vehicles on the gravel made him return to the window. First one police car drove through the gates, then another, then a third. He went and sat back on the bed; there was a hammering on the bedroom door.

'But it's not me. I'm not him.' Roger Mace knew the choking, the nausea, the chest pain was returning. The officer glanced at his colleague and shook his head.

In his office, the Superintendent put down the folder and looked at the Inspector. 'Run it past me again.'

'The body is that of Gabriela Fuentes, wife of Marco Arcardi, y'know, owns that football club. It was common knowledge, in the classical music world that is, that she and Steffan Bergman were lovers. She disappeared about two years ago; had been living in

Madrid. One day, told her maid she was going shopping and never came home. The maid knew of the affair and never reported it, until the husband, who had been in America wanted to know her whereabouts. Of course, the maid had known nothing, or so she said.'

The Superintendent made his usual whistle through his teeth.

'Did the husband make any effort to find her? Was it in the news?

'Dunno, sir. They had what is called an open marriage.'

'But all the same … and Bergman what had he been doing?

'But he says he's not Bergman.'

'Forget that. What do we actually know about Bergman?'

'He suddenly gave up the tours. Last one was in Sydney. Now lives a quiet life … bit of a recluse I think.'

The Superintendent interrupted, 'Have we anything else on the woman?'

The Inspector said: 'Forensics believe she's been dead for about two years.'

'That fits.'

'The body had been hidden in a cupboard at the back of the garage. The fire burnt through the wood and, hey presto, she fell out.'

The Superintendent was going to comment on his Inspector's use of language, but let it go.

The Inspector thought he ought to move the conversation on. 'The guy ... I mean the man we're holding claims he is not Steffan Bergman.'

'Then who is he?'

'Don't know. Won't say. Though he claimed to be Bergman when we first arrived. Then said he wasn't when he found out about the body.'

'He's playing for time.'

The Inspector laughed, 'That's good sir. Playing for time, like playing the piano.'

The Superintendent didn't look up, but said: 'Well, he looks like Bergman; he's living in Bergman's house. He's been seen driving Bergman's car ... and if he's not Bergman. Where is Bergman?'

'Don't know, sir.'

'And who is this guy?'

'Don't know, sir.'

The Superintendent stared at the Inspector.

All that night in the cell, Roger made one decision after another, immediately discarding them all. When a plan began to take shape, he felt the tightness easing in his ribs; his breathing slowed, but no ... a stupid idea and the shaking started again.

The Inspector said, 'He's not Bergman. We've finger-printed him and it's a Roger Albert Mace; had him for thieving from large houses a few years back.'

'So where is Bergman?'

'Don't know, sir.'

The Superintendent's thin whistle floated across the desk. 'Charge Roger Albert Mace with the murder of Steffan Bergman _and_ Gabriela Fuentes.'

'Yes, sir.' "

'How do you know all this?' I asked.

He shrugged his shoulders; then smiled.

*

10th Story

I had dropped my spoon and was scrabbling under the table when I heard him say, 'Are you okay?'

I pulled myself up onto my chair, 'Hello. Haven't seen you in ages.'

'Just back from India.'

'India? Lucky you.'

'Yes; been to see my brother.'

I found a tissue in my bag, wiped the spoon and stirred my cappuccino.

'I usually try and visit him once a year.

I waited until he had been served his tea and said, 'And …'

'He works for a charity in Mumbai.'

'And …'

He laughed, 'And what?'

'Come on; don't tease. You must have a story for me.'

'Funny you should say that; I have got a tale my brother told me.'

I took a sip of my coffee, 'Yes?'

He poured out his tea, smiled and said:

"The Silent Temple …

As you know, when the world was new, the great god Vishnu took three huge strides across the universe, and the Milky Way fell from the sky; and each falling star turned into a drop of water, and the water became the River Ganges.

Now on the banks of this sacred river, a little limestone temple was built for the villagers to worship Ganesha, the Elephant-god of wisdom and good fortune. All was well for many, many years until a strange and frightening event occurred – the temple bell ceased to ring … and it happened like this:

One morning, the purjari, the priest who lived in the temple, and led the worship, had risen before dawn to collect water from the sacred river. He mixed the water with milk and carefully washed Ganesha. The purjari then covered Ganesha in sandalwood paste and placed a garland of flowers around his neck. As the sun rose, the villagers arrived at the temple and the purjari pulled back the curtains of the shrine in readiness. Ready for that special moment when the worshippers saw Ganesha. That special moment was darshem. The purjari could hear the villagers outside the shrine removing their shoes. The first through the temple doorway was Jayaraj; the oldest man in the village, his hand outstretched offering Ganesha a grain of rice. Jayaraj paused and lifted the other hand to the hanging bell. He touched the bell and listened for the chime. The chime that would wake Ganesha. But in the shrine room there was silence. The old man touched the bell again and watched it swing, but again, silence. The purjari swung the bell, but not a sound. Jayaraj cried and fell to the floor; he pulled at his beard; he beat his head. Two young men heard his cries and dragged him out of the temple, past the bewildered villagers and left him sobbing under the banyan tree.

How the word spread. Soon everyone knew that the temple bell was silent. The purjari could not make it ring. The great Pandit Rama, the wisest priest in the temple, could not make it ring. If Pandit Rama could not make the bell chime what was to do? How was the villagers ever going to wake Ganesha if the bell stayed silent? If Ganesha was asleep, how was he going to receive their gifts of flower petals and little sweetmeats and hear their prayers? The villagers needed to practice puja towards the Elephant-god, for besides being the god of wisdom and good fortune, he had to be honoured before a new venture was undertaken – and there were always new ventures: planting seeds; harvesting crops; a journey to the next village; arranging a wedding.

Life in the village was sombre. Early every morning purjari still washed Ganesha, covered him in sandalwood paste, and opened the curtains, but the Elephant-god did not wake. As was said, not to hear the temple bell ring, was strange and frightening. Mothers swept their homes in silence. Daughters did not chatter at the well, and even the boys stopped shying stones at the chickens. And every day, old Jayaraj sat under the banyan tree with his head bowed.

Then old day, Jayaraj hobbled up to the temple and spoke to Pandit Rama. When Jayaraj had finished Pandit Rama put his palms together and said:

'I agree. Go.'

The villagers watched Jayaraj bundle up his belongings, close the door of his hut and leave the village.

The moon grew and dimished a hundred times before Jayaraj returned. One morning just as the sky was lightening to a pale grey, he returned and went straight to the temple. Then the villagers heard it. The bell was ringing; a silver sound chimed from the temple. The purjari came out and ushered the villagers up to the shrine. Ganesha, garlanded in yellow and pink flowers sat awake; ready to receive puja.

So, how had Jayaraj made the temple bell ring again? This is what happened – the old man had travelled to the city and prayed at the shrine of Vishnu. Vishnu had listened, then gave him a tiny star from the Milky Way and told him what to do. Once, home again in the village, Jayaraj went to the temple and gave the star to the purjari. The purjari had tossed it into the air. The star fell onto the bell and the bell rang out once more.

The strange and frightening time was gone. Mothers smiled and sang as they swept their homes; the girls laughed and chatted by the well and the boys chased the chickens again. Now the temple bell always rings and the villages can always honour their Elephant-god Ganesha."

'Magical,' I said, and clinked the side of my cup with the spoon.

He smiled, 'I heard that.'

*

11th Story

As the waitress put down my cappuccino, the coffee slopped into the saucer; I looked at her, but she obviously hadn't noticed and walked away. I was scrapping the bottom of the cup along the saucer's edge when he came up to the table and said,   'Hold on I'll get a paper napkin.'

He returned and sat down.

'Thanks,'

I put the napkin in the saucer and waited for it to soak up the coffee. He busied himself with his tea when it was served.

How are things?' I asked.

'Fine. My god-son's birthday at the end of the week.

He took a cheque book and pen from his jacket pocket, 'Have bought the card and I just want to enclose a cheque for him.'

'You use a fountain pen?' I said.

He smiled. 'I know, but at least it's not a quill.'

When he had finished writing, I said, 'May I look at the pen.'

'It's very ordinary, but was my father's.'

It was black; the cap was chipped and the silver clasp loose. He looked at it for a moment when I handed it back.

'Come on, 'I said,' You're thinking and I know what that means.'

He smiled and said:

"The Fountain Pen ...

The Senior Manager moved it with the point of his pencil – it spun round on the shiny surface of the closed laptop. He flicked it again – this time more sharply so that as it turned, it slid off onto the desk. The Senior Manager left it where it was – fingerprints?

'Smith. Brian. Can you explain?'

Brian knew a line of sweat was slipping between his shoulder blades; his armpits were sticky. He looked at the fountain pen; slim; elegant; the gold bands and clip enhancing the mother-of-pearl. Was it only yesterday he first saw it, admired it, wanted it, took it?

Reflecting on the entire episode Brian blamed his glands.

It had been quite unnecessary for the woman to slam the bell to attract his attention; she was only standing across the counter from him.

'Good afternoon Madam.'

'All right darling?'

'May I help you Madam?'

Her laugh was deep and throaty: 'I'd be disappointed if you can't.'

'Madam; do you wish to book into the hotel?'

The woman opened her pink patent leather handbag. 'Give me a light, there's a good boy.'

'We have a single, with supplement of course.'

'God no! – don't you have a suite?'

Brian rattled the keyboard and looked at the screen.

'We have the Cleopatra Suite.'

The woman leaned over and rapped his knuckles with the cigarette holder.

'You may book me into that – three days. Now give me a light, do.'

Brian pointed to the large black and red sign above his head. 'Sorry Madam. Smoking is only permitted over there in the small side lounge.'

The woman winked and Brian stood mesmerised by the rhythmic seesawing of her buttocks as she sauntered across the vestibule. She had left her handbag open on the counter. Brian tore his eyes from her backside and peered into the bag. He noticed a mobile phone, wallet, keys, lipstick and some paper tissues. On the tissues was a pen – a fountain pen and … Wow! What a pen! Brian's fingers nipped it out of the bag. It was shimmering amethyst interlaced with turquoise; the clip, gold filigree. Brian slowly unscrewed the cap and the nib twinkled up at him. Brian sat at his desk; found a notepad and began signing his name. The pen's iridescent colours changed from mauve and sea green as his hand moved. The deep violet ink encouraged him to add flourishes to his signature. *Brian Smith. Bryan Smith. Bryan Smythe. Bryan Theodore Smythe. Bryan Smythe Esquire. The Hon. Bryan Smythe, MP. The Earl of Smytheto…*

The heavy laugh sang across to the reception desk. Brian jumped up; rammed the cap back on the pen and just as his hand reached the bag, the woman swung it from the counter and over her shoulder. She smiled at Brian.

'See about my luggage sweetie.'

'First your registration, Madam.'

Brian admired his cool authoritative tone. The pen was burning in his trouser pocket. He looked down at the keyboard; the letters were jumbling; his fingers shaking.

He was off duty by six thirty, but remained behind the desk fidgeting and shuffling and annoying the Night Manager. He saw her come down the staircase, clacking her heels on each marble tread, then swayed herself round the carved urn on the last step. He waited another few minutes after she had gone through to the dining room, and while the Night Manager booked in a couple, took the pass key, shot through the staff door, up the concrete back stairs to the fourth floor. He pushed open the door and stepped onto the extravagantly carpeted corridor. He stood by the archway leading to the Cleopatra Suite.

'Anything wrong Smith?'

The Senior Manager was by his side waiting for Brian to speak.

'No-o-o, I thought …'

'I do not want to find you where you should not be; that understood?'

Brian nodded and walked away towards the lift.

'Back stairs Smith, if you don't mind.'

Down in the staff rest room, Brian debated his problem. His intention of leaving the pen on the floor of the Cleopatra Suite and her assuming it had fallen from her bag had been fine if it hadn't been for Mr Snoops – what was he doing up there anyway? He could get rid of it; go out and drop it in a street bin, but the thought of it tossed around with half eaten burgers, empty crisp packets and worse, being stuck up against a blob of unwanted chewing gum, was not what his fastidious nature could accept. No; he would return it to her handbag – alone in the security of the rest room he felt able to take on the challenge. He smirked. Yes, quite a challenge. He was up to it. He slid through to the reception area and lolled against the desk; the Night Manager ignored him. It struck nine; from the dining room, the clatter and hum had died down. He watched a waiter carry a tray of coffee into the main lounge, and followed. She was sitting alone on sofa; she'd kicked off her shoes, her head rested on the cushions and her eyes were closed. The bag was by her toes. Brian put a finger to his lips and took a coffee cup from the waiter; the waiter shrugged and carried the tray across to a group sitting by the fireplace. Brian placed the coffee on the low table; he squatted near the bag and put his hand in his pocket, his fingers gripped the pen as with his other hand he tugged at the clasp on the bag. The bag moved; it brushed against her foot. She opened her eyes and pushed herself from the cushions.

'Coffee. Thank you darling.'

The next morning, as breakfast was being served and Brian was finalising the bills, he saw her go into the dining room.

He had sat up late in his room last night using the pen; he was mesmerised by it. He laid it on his palm and as he moved his hand watched the colours roll from lilac to purple; cream to rose; blue to green. He filled two pages of his diary signing his name with more loops and curls.

Antonio, the trainee Manager, skidded across the vestibule to the reception desk. Brian looked at the clock. 'Will you be able to manage on your own for a while?' he asked.

'Sure man. Me okay.'

Brian blew out his cheeks and shook his head.

She was sitting in an alcove and the bag hung over the back of her chair. He pushed past a family leaving and stood by her table.

'Madam – is your stay here to your satisfaction?'

She forked a piece of bacon and a mushroom and dipped it into the egg yolk. She swallowed, then cut the end off the sausage and spiked it to half a tomato. Brian put his hand on the back of her chair and leaned forward.

'Anything we can do to make your stay …'

'Smith, you again.' The Senior Manager's smile ran round the room.

Brian's fingers fumbled with the handbag's straps. The Senior Manager gripped Brian's elbow, 'Outside. Now.'

She waved her fork at them both, 'Everything is perfect.'

In the vestibule Brian heard Antonio checking out a guest. The Senior Manager looked at Brian. 'Get over there and sort it.'

Brian smoothed out the problem and walked the guest to the revolving doors. On the pavement the guest flagged down a taxi and a police car pulled up.

The Senior Manager, Deputy Manager, Bella, the Senior House-keeper were all squashed into the back office.

Brian had stood obliging and helpful at the reception desk; he'd seen her leave the dining room and wait for the lift; a man followed her into the lift. Brian knew it wasn't a guest. Antonio was nowhere to be seen; five then ten minutes passed before he appeared.

'You wanted,' Antonio pointed to the closed office door.

'What do you mean?' asked Brian.

'Important. Very. You wanted.'

Brian was irritated; little runt ordering him around.

The room was crowded and stuffy. Besides the hotel staff was a man and woman with *police* written all over their plain clothes.

'Ah, Smith; just a question or two.' It was the Deputy Manager who spoke.

Brian looked for an empty chair; there wasn't one.

'Cleopatra Suite,' butted in the Senior Manager, 'Why were you …'

Brian felt a trickle of sweat by his ear, he pulled out his handkerchief and the pen flew and twisted from his pocket like a sequinned trapeze artist. It landed on the closed laptop and that was when the Senior Manager spun it with the point of his pencil.

***

'You tell me more. You tell me all.'

The Night Manager put his feet up on the reception desk and bit into a cheese and pickle sandwich. Antonio took the other half of the sandwich, opened it, then put it back on the plate.

The Night Manager mumbled, 'She had all the stuff in her luggage.'

'What stuff?'

'Bella told me. She saw it all. Watches, necklaces, bracelets, all sorts of jewellery. She does the shop lifting, then hands it over to the guy. Big hotel like this – plenty of comings and goings.'

'And Mr Smith?'

'Oh, Brian? He was obviously the look-out, the go-between.'

Antonio yawned, 'How you mean go-between?'

The Night Manager brushed crumbs from his waistcoat, 'Are you going to eat this other sandwich?'

Antonio shook his head and yawned again.

'What I want to know,' the Night Manager tossed a crust onto the plate, 'Is why did Mr Brian Clever Smith keep that pen? Seems crazy. We've got loads of Biros here.' "

I said, 'Look after your pen.'
He smiled, 'I will.'

*

12th Story

I had just been served my cappuccino when I noticed him standing by the table.

May I?'

'Certainly.'

The waitress brought his tea and we both sipped our drinks, the silence between us was companionable.

'Shall I tell you where I went yesterday evening?' I said.

'Please do.'

'School Reunion.'

He groaned. 'Oh, no. Poor you.'

'Exactly. Girls' Convent School. What a fool; spent the evening surrounded by all that success.'

'I was a border in Wales.'

'Even worse.'

'True; though I enjoyed primary school.'

I said, 'Yes, me too. Lovely teachers. One in particular was my favourite.

'I know a little story about a teacher.'
'Tell me.'
He smiled and said:

"The Lesson …

Raymond loved Miss Donovan. Loved her with all his heart. He loved her smooth, white hands. He loved her happy smile. Her shining black shoes with the little heels that clicked, clicked across the classroom floor. He loved the way she spoke his name when calling the Register. He waited all through the 'Bs' and 'Cs', one 'E' and two 'Gs', then 'Hopkins' – her voice changed he was sure - 'Hopkins'. But most of all her loved her hair. It was the colour of … buttered toast.

Standing by Miss Donovan's desk as she marked his exercise book, he was so near that he could see the little golden loops on her neck; whispery coils around her ears. Miss Donovan wore he hair piled up; it was like a … soft cushion thought Raymond. Studying the twists and curls that had escaped from the combs Raymond would be oblivious of her talking. She would close the book and, smiling, hand it back to him. Raymond would start; guilty at staring so closely. Miss Donovan would say: 'Back to your desk, Dreamer.'

It was the last afternoon of term. Miss Donovan had finished telling the story, but the bell hadn't rung. Miss Donovan looked at her watch, patted her lap with her palms as though she had come to a decision. Raymond was dreaming. He had heard the first part of the story – about wild horses and the bandit, but then he gazed out of the window. Looking up to the summer sky, he could see the gable end of the school roof. Strutting along the ridge was a pigeon. Raymond watched with envy its sure-footedness. Forward, turn, pause, back, pause, turn, forward. If only he could balance like that. And the view. If that pigeon really wanted, he could look down onto the mound of coke behind the playground. Raymond would have loved to glimpse that coke mountain – that would be the bestest …the most …

The 'Oooooo Miss' and 'Aaaaaahh' that breathed around the room made Raymond turned away from the window. He looked across the gang-way at the two girls in the next desk. They were open-mouthed. Raymond swivelled and looked behind, first at Barry Groves and then along the expanse of amazed expressions of all the class. One or two girls giggled. Raymond prodded Barry Groves in the chest.

'Oi', Barry shoved Raymond's arm away and pointed.

Miss Donovan was standing by the blackboard; her golden hair cascading like a shimmering cloak over her arms and shoulders. Miss Donovan laughed and shook her head from side to side making the tresses sway and curve across her face. One moment her smile was there, the next hidden as though by a curtain of amber silk. Miss Donovan laughed again, tossed back her head and the hair swung and fell in soft waves down her back.

'There,' said Miss Donovan to the class, 'That's our secret.' She reached up to the nape of her neck, pulled the hair forward and coiled it like a rope.

'Miss.' squealed Raymond. He had stood up. The class, jolted out of their adventure by the piercing cry, turned and stared. Raymond fell back onto his seat. Miss Donovan stepped towards him.

'M-i-s-s.' gulped Raymond. He dropped his chin and squeezed shut his eyes to prevent those hot little bubbles from running down his face. Miss Donovan stooped down in front of him. With one hand she held the desk-lid for balance; with the other she lightly shook his arm.

'Raymond?' Come on. What is the matter? Last day of term. Holidays tomorrow.'

Then the loving tears exploded from his heart. He flung himself at her. 'You're so l-o-v-e-l-y,' he sobbed.

Miss Donovan gently pushed him away into his seat. Her hair clung to his wet cheeks making a veil between them. Raymond reached out. He looped his fingers through the soft, satiny web and curved his hand so that the hair wound around his fist like a warm glove. Miss Donovan slowly tugged her hair away and brushed it from Raymond's face. As Miss Donovan stood up, the bell jangled along the corridor and the strange magic of the afternoon turned into the romping delight of the summer holidays.

***

The classroom smelt of tidiness and new exercise books. The door opened and the class stood and chanted: 'Good morning Miss Donovan.'

She smiled. 'Good morning class. Sit down please.'

She stepped across the room, put the Register on the table and turned to the children. 'I have a different name now. My name is Mrs Whittaker.' She held up her hand and the class looked at the narrow gold ring on her finger.

Mrs Whittaker took a new piece of chalk from the box and wrote on the backboard. *'Today is the start of a new beginning.'*

Raymond watched. He had watched as she came into the room and stood smiling. He had watched her walk, click, click, click across to her table. He had watched her wave her new wedding ring at the class. He watched her soft white hand moving across the blackboard. He looked at her hair – her short cropped hair; fitting her head like a tight cap. Around her ears instead of those tiny, twisting curls were sharp bristles. Coils, like golden springs on her neck were gone. Her forehead was a hidden by a fringe – straight and severe.

***

In the Kitchen, Mrs Hopkins had just finished making the tea as Raymond opened the back door.

'Hello love. How was school?'

Raymond threw his satchel down by the cooker. 'Srrallright.'

'And your Miss Donovan?

Raymond looked at the plate of buttered toast on the kitchen table.

'How was she today?'

Raymond picked up a piece of toast. With his mouth full, he mumbled: 'It's Mrs Whittaker now … Miss Donovan has gone.' "

I looked at him.

'Are you Raymond?' I asked.

He shook his head and smiled.

*

13th Story

The waitress served me my cappuccino; I thanked her and was checking my watch when he pushed through the door and said, 'May I join you, or are you in a hurry?'

'No, I was just wondering if I was too late for my cappuccino.'

He gave me a little frown, 'Oh, yes?'

'I've read that Italians do not believe you should drink cappuccino after 11am – some say 10am. It is a breakfast drink only.'

He smiled, 'Okay.'

The waitress put his tea on the table.

'But tea can be drunk at any time,' I continued.

'Okay,' he said again, 'Have you got a busy day?'

'I've joined an Art History Course. First lesson today is Italian Painting.'

'Hence your thoughts about how the Italians drink their coffee.'

'True,' I agreed.

He took a sip of his tea and said, 'Where I used to live there was a Museum that housed some marvellous Italian paintings. It was when I was a student and I'd spend much of my time in the Museum.'

'We're you studying art?'

'No, I used to go there on wintery afternoons to keep warm.'

I drank some of my cappuccino, 'Have you a story about a painting? Please - I think I'll need all the help I can get for this art course.'

He smiled and said:

"The Mother and the Child …

The museum attendant watched the woman walk slowly but determinedly to the archway – her shoes not making a sound on the marble floor.

'Here she is; dead on time.'

He noticed her shoulder bag – the kind you pick up in a native market – a woven kaleidoscope of colours. 'Strange,' he thought.

During the weeks he had been observing the woman, she never carried a bag. As the woman passed under the archway, the attendant stood up, stretched his arms, waited, then with a discreet nod to a colleague, followed. The woman stood, as usual, in the centre of the room; her head tipped back, then she slowly turned round and round looking at the painted ceiling. Despite knowing exactly what the woman was seeing, the attendant too glanced up at the cherubs peering from clouds, soft and white; angels in gold and cerise robes trumpeting amongst the blue canopy of heavenly bliss and wonderment.

When the attendant looked down, the woman had gone. 'Again strange,' he mused. He knew from past observation the woman always took three to four minutes studying the ceiling. 'What's she up to?'

He hurried from the room into the Long Gallery and spotted her sitting on a bench. There was an unfamiliar pattern to her behaviour today that he was unsure about. He waited. He woman stood up and sauntered down the Long Gallery pausing to look intently at each of her reflections in the ornate wall mirrors. When she reached the Grand Staircase she turned and looked back. 'Damn,' thought the attendant, 'She's twigged.'

Suddenly the woman began running down the staircase; her hand sliding along the polished banister for balance; the bag swinging against her hip. At the bottom of the stairs she looked up, then walked past the Egyptology gallery and into the room displaying the work of the Quattrocento artists.

When the attendant reached the room, the woman was sitting on the bench looking at the picture. He sighed. He felt relieved. What the little escapade upstairs had been about he didn't know, but this was normal. There she was: as always: looking at the picture.

The attendant was an ambitious young man who kept his ears and eyes open for any vagaries amongst the public that would promote him away from the six and a half hours daily patrolling. He stood in the doorway staring into the middle distance. He had no need to look at the painting; he had studied it enough times – every day when the woman left the room, he would stand in front of the picture and try to fathom just what it was in the subject that held the woman's attention. It was of the Madonna –wearing not a blue veil, but a golden brown shawl; both round her shoulders and over the child. Her hand supported the child's head; his eyes drooping ready for sleep. Her face was bent towards the child; ringlets of hair against her cheek.

Now the woman, usually as still as a sculpture began to fidget: she hugged her arms across her chest; she turned on the bench; she pulled at her bag. The attendant shifted his feet – ready – and waited. He noticed she had closed her eyes and was murmuring to herself. He moved closer. She was singing. Gently rocking backwards and forwards, singing softly. He listened. It was a lullaby. Sweet and lyrical, but then the attendant heard a sob. He looked away; he felt an intruder.

The woman's scream made the attendant flinch and as he did so, the woman lunged at the picture. A flash of knowing satisfaction passed through the attendant's mind as he ran to the wall and slammed his palm against the security button. He jumped towards the woman and swung out his arm to grab her. She stared at him; her face distorted as though in pain; the attendant dropped his arm and backed away. He watched her shake her head and return to the bench. She was singing the lullaby again when the security guards arrived. The woman's bag was searched and the attendant recorded with date and time: 03.04.13 – 16.55 its contents: a red purse holding £2.76 and a Yale key; a neatly folded man's handkerchief and a silver photo frame. The attendant was surprised at not finding a knife, scissors. nor a tin of paint; any of the usual items used for destroying works of art. The woman snatched back the purse and handkerchief. The photo frame slipped from her trembling fingers. The attendant picked it up. On the back was a date: 3rd April 2003. He turned it over; it was empty – there was no photo – just a framed square of cream cardboard.

The woman had been taken away and it was a few minutes before the museum closed. The attendant went back into the room and looked again at the painting. Usual sort of thing for that time in art history: Madonna and Child. No signature, so possibly from a *school*. He looked closer at the Madonna's face – looked at the eyes.

'Mmm,' he straightened up, 'Never noticed that before.'

The attendant went through to the staff room to collect his coat. When he walked under the archway, he stopped and looked for a moment at the painted ceiling. The figures still and silent: but were they? Were they watching – recording – remembering

'Now don't start getting fanciful', he told himself.

It had rained, but now, just as it was easing off, the late sun dazzled the wet pavement. It was when he reached the Underground station that he heard a rumble of thunder. He looked up and was surprised to see a sky as bright and colourful as the painted ceiling. The attendant paused before stepping into the booking hall and that was when the lightning forked and struck."

I didn't say anything, just finished my cappuccino.

He smiled; lifted his cup then saw that he had drunk all his tea.

*

14th Story

I hadn't drunk any of my cappuccino when I heard him say,

'Are you all right?

'Yes, thank you. Sort of. Just taken flowers to my father's grave.'

'Sorry.'

'My mother insists on certain flowers and they are not always in season, and some she doesn't like – she thinks they are superstitious; having meanings, you know'

'I understand.'

'Cheer me up with a story,' I said.

The waitress set down his teapot, cup and saucer.

'Or haven't you got one.'

He leaned back in his chair; tapped his fingers on the table for a moment, smiled and said:

"Flowers for the Future …

Philip laid his palm against the deep maroon paintwork and pushed at the door. Though it was February, the early morning sunlight had warmed the panels. The door scratched over the flag stones of the porch. The double glass doors into the church were propped open and he trotted down the disabled ramp. He stood for a moment in the greyness and remembered. Forty-one years ago. He heard the soft tinkle as the clock struck half-past. As his eyes grew accustomed to the gloom he thought the church was empty, then a wall light flickered on and he noticed the vicar; the fabric of his emerald green cope shone like a jewel. The vicar gave a slight nod and pointed to the grand piano by the font. Philip walked towards it and saw a pile of Order of Service books. He took a copy then noticed a few people sitting in pews along the side aisle. He walked quickly down the narrow aisle and reached a back pew just as the vicar passed him and stepped up to the altar.

Philip opened the Order of Service book; the priest welcomed the congregation then in a subdued voice read from the book. Philip tried to follow the words, but tears jumped and blurred the letters. He kept his head bowed and tugged a handkerchief from his pocket. He became aware of movement; people in front were shuffling hassocks and kneeling. He thought his joints wouldn't let him get down, never mind up again. He leaned forward, rested his elbows on his knees and cradled his head in his hands. He closed his eyes and saw himself and Carol walking down centre aisle, rain splattering against the windows and the wind crashing open the porch door; Sadie, the smallest bridesmaid, skipping between them and Carol turning, catching her hand.

Philip realised people were in the aisle queuing towards the altar. He stood, sat down again, then after a moment or two joined the end of the queue. When there was a space at the altar rail, Philip gritted his teeth and knelt. 'Please God, let me be able to get up again.' He knew if Carol had been there she would have dug him in the ribs and said: *'Naughty. Not that sort of prayer.'* He glanced up and saw the heavy brocade; hands in front of his face holding the white disc. 'The body of Christ.' Philip opened his mouth and tasted the smooth nothingness of the wafer. He tried to swallow, but a morsel caught in his throat. 'Please God don't let me choke.' He heard Carol tut-tutting. He knew the chalice would be heavy, so lightly touched the base indicating to the vicar not to let go. He looked at wine; the deep red liquid shimmered; then his lips touched the cold silver rim. 'The blood of Christ.'

It was only him kneeling. He gripped the rail, got a purchase on his shoes, pushed down then stood. He waited for a moment until the cream-washed walls steadied, and went back to his seat.

Through the vicar's ritual of completing the Communion – rinsing of the chalice, folding the white linen cloth, Philip watched. Above the altar the blue, stained-glass dress of the Virgin grew brighter by the minute. Shafts of sunbeams glistened on the vicar's bald head. Everyone was leaving; voices mumbled. Philip waited; he didn't want to talk to anyone, but then the pew began to feel hard and uncomfortable and he thought someone might be waiting to lock up. As he walked along the aisle he noticed the head of a flower on the slabs. He picked it up, it was a narcissus; though one or two of the outer white petals looked tired, the yellow corona was fresh and Philip tucked the flower into the breast pocket of his jacket and said: 'Good morning' to the verger who was fidgeting with a bunch of keys.

The next month, March, Philip felt more sure of himself; he quickly took the Order of Service book and a place in an empty pew. At first he followed the vicar's words more closely, then watched the coloured windows grow dim and realised it was raining; he thought about their wedding photographer trying to side-step a puddle on the churchyard path and Carol giggling when he didn't succeed. He could see Carol's veil flying in the wind.

When he left, a woman was pushing backwards through the porch doors; Philip held the doors for her.   She smiled,' Many thanks.' over the bunch of tulips she was carrying. 'Service finished?'

'Yes.'

'I try and get the flowers done before the service, but I'm definitely running late today.' She smiled again. Philip nodded, 'Bye.'

It was one of those perfect brand-new April mornings. The sky was fresh, the air just warm and, Philip said to himself: no litter in the churchyard. In the porch the woman had lifted the flower arrangement ready to take through to the church. She said 'Good morning.'

Philip said: My wife carried freesias on our wedding day.'

Why did I blurt that out? he thought.

The woman put down the flowers. 'My, you're clever to remember. Most men can't recall anything about their wedding day.'

'They were white,' continued Philip. He saw Carol holding the small bunch, decorated with trailing green as they were being driven from the church to the reception. She had said: 'Freesias; they mean *Thoughtfulness*.' And he had kissed her.

The woman continued: 'White freesias. Must have looked lovely. I chose yellow today. I thought yellow was just right for this spring morning. Sorry, but I mustn't keep you.'

Philip followed her into the church. She put the freesias by the font; their bright gold a contrast against the grey stone. Philip collected an Order of Service sheet and found a seat.

The next time, Philip noticed the flowers straight away. Agapanthus; huge clusters of deep blue blossom reached across the covered font; their big, round blooms stretching strong and wide. Philip was aware of someone by his side and a whisper, 'Not too extravagant, do you think?'

Philip turned, smiled and shook his head. He didn't see her after the service, but he was now on nodding 'Good morning' terms to several of the congregation and sauntered down to the lych gate with a middle-aged couple who told him about their Jack Russell puppy.

The arrangement for June was delphiniums. Stems of soft blue, and to his mind, a gentle flower. He remembered that there had been delphiniums in the garden of their first house; then one year they never bloomed. He thought back: Carol had talked about buying more plants, but life had got in the way and then they had moved. After the service he saw her collecting together secateurs, oasis, vases.

'Need help?' he asked.

'Yes please. Just taking them to the car.'

Philip carried a box for her, and told her about the lost delphiniums all those years ago.

'Yes, that can happen.'

They stood for a moment, the sun warming their shoulders. Philip said: 'Such a warm morning. Would you like to sit for a moment. Sorry; are you in a hurry?'

She smiled. 'That would be perfect. I have got a few chores waiting to be done, so thank you for suggesting I put them off for a while.'

They found a bench, set in an alcove on the west side of the. Philip knew he shouldn't keep talking about himself, but couldn't help it, and she was such a good listener; he noticed the way she folded her hands in her lap. He told her about Carol's death; her illness; visiting her grave. He stopped as the word 'bore' flashed into his mind. The woman smiled.

'You told me a little about your wedding. Your wife carried freesias?'

'Yes.'

'Mmm. Lovely for you to have such memories – keep them safe.'

The woman glanced away. 'Mine was a Registry Office affair. Didn't last.'

'Oh.'

'Many years ago now. Nearly all forgotten.' She smiled again and stood up. 'Nice talking to you.'

'You too,' said Philip.

Philip missed the next monthly Eucharist; he had his cousin staying. Roy had discovered a coach trip from Solihull to Norfolk.

'So, I'll come for a week. No problem at all,' said Roy. Philip sighed and agreed. Roy was an organiser and a time keeper. He'd planned a day out by train for them both, and Philip knew, as he suggested it, that it was pointless to talk of a later train so he could go to the church service.

'No. No. Would upset the complete schedule of the day,' said Roy. Philip sighed and agreed.

'Sweet peas,' said Philip.

'Like them?' asked the woman.

Philip stood by the font; the perfume masked the church's usual mustiness.

'Wonderful colours aren't they? It's August and they have been constantly flowering for weeks. Must like that part of my garden.'

Philip nodded.

'Mauve, white, purple, pink. Can never make up my mind the shade I like the most.'

Philip nodded.

The clock struck the half past and the vicar stepped from the vestry. Philip smiled at the woman and followed the vicar along the aisle. The woman was waiting for him after the service. She handed him a small posy of the sweet peas.

'Thought you may like these ... for your wife's ... for the grave.'

Philip told himself to stop being stupid and blinked away the mistiness in his eyes.

The next month, the first thing Philip noticed was how desolate the font looked without any flowers. As he was leaving he asked,

'The lady that does the flowers. Is she away?'

The verger overheard his query, 'Stroke,' he said locking up the Order of Service books in the cupboard.

Again there were no flowers by the font when Philip went to the October Eucharist. At the end of the service he waited by the vestry door and caught the vicar's eye.

'The lady who usually does the flowers ...' he pointed to the font.

'Mrs Bennett? Still in hospital. She was included in our prayers this morning.'

'Yes, um, I didn't know her name.'

'No. Not in hospital. Moved to a convalescent home. The Grange – just by the park.'

The vicar gave Philip a tight dismissive smile.

It was the last of the lavender that Philip had picked from the bush next to the back door; it had looked a fine bunch on the draining board, but seemed a poor, pathetic arrangement as he handed them to Mrs Bennett. She was sitting by the French windows, saw him across the room and waved.

'How clever of you to find me.'

'Well, I asked.'

'And how clever of you to bring me lavender – it means *Good Luck*. Did you know?'

Philip shook his head.

'And I have been very lucky. I'm really on the mend.'

'I'm so pleased Mrs Bennett … I'

'It's Rose,' she laughed, 'Another flower.'

By November, Rose was fit, strong and home again. She and Philip's friendship jogged along in a companionable way. They shared many things: a liking for Scrabble; TV detective series Mozart – a dislike of modern art; tattoos, especially on girls' legs. Rose was a good cook; far better than Carol.

'Sorry, love, but it's true,' he told her photograph.

Rose's Tuesday invitation to lunch helped him through the week, but what Philip admired most in Rose was her pleasure in hearing about Philip's marriage to Carol.

'Are you sure you don't mind my talking about it?' he asked on more than one occasion.

'Phil,' (he was happy with his name's diminutive) I might not have had a good marriage, but that doesn't mean I don't want to hear about others.'

Another aspect of their joint friendship was the visits to garden centres choosing flowers for Rose's monthly floral arrangement.

It was the following October. Philip said, 'Are you busy next Sunday?'

'N-o-o-o.'

'I would like to take you out to lunch. A special lunch. Celebrate a whole year of our friendship.'

Rose was ready when the taxi pulled up and she watched Philip fumble from the car and open the gate.

'What is he carrying,' she thought.

When she opened the front door, she laughed, 'Is it you? Are you there?'

Philip handed Rose the two bunches of chrysanthemums. The copper petals gleamed as she carried them into the kitchen.

'Thank you, Phil,' she said, 'Must put them in water. They are really beautiful.'

'I thought,' said Philip, 'One bunch for you and one for the church ... if you think that is okay.'

'Phil, how clever of you.'

Two days later Philip pushed open the porch door, trotted down the ramp and collected his Order of Service book. He looked across at the font; the burnished chrysanthemums looked polished and majestic. Rose came and stood by him. 'Do you know what chrysanthemums represent?' she whispered.

Philip shook his head.

'Optimism,'

Philip took Rose's hand and together they found an empty pew."

'Sorry, being stupid,' I said sniffing.

I started to drink my cappuccino and he smiled and patted my arm.

*

Dear Reader

If you have enjoyed reading this book, then
please leave a review on Amazon.

Thank you.

About The Author

With this, her second book, Pam Finch has drawn on a selection of her writings to produce this compilation of reflective and entertaining stories.

If you enjoyed "Cappuccino Moments" you may like to read her first book, "Minho Moments", a collection of stories set in secluded mountain hamlets, seaside villages and the bustling city of Porto.

ISBN: 978-1512151602

To find out more about Pam, or to follow her on social media, visit:

Facebook: https://www.facebook.com/Pam-Finch-419302668258737/?fref=ts

Blog: https://pamfinchwriter.wordpress.com/

www.ingramcontent.com/pod-product-compliance
Lightning Source LLC
Chambersburg PA
CBHW060435130626
46555CB00005B/2373